THE DASTARDLY DRAGON KILLER AND THE POISON BREATH

POINT MUSE COZY PARANORMAL MYSTERY: BOOK TWO

KELLY ETHAN

Copyright © 2020 by Kelly Ethan

All rights reserved.

No part of this book may be reproduced in any form or by any electronic or mechanical means, including information storage and retrieval systems, without written permission from the author, except for the use of brief quotations in a book review.

Publisher's Note: This is a work of fiction. Names, characters, places, and incidents are a product of the author's imagination. Locales and public names are sometimes used for atmospheric purposes. Any resemblance to actual people, living or dead, or to businesses, companies, events, institutions, or locales is completely coincidental.

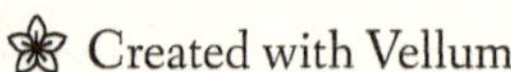 Created with Vellum

THE DASTARDLY DRAGON KILLER
AND THE POISON BREATH -
BOOK TWO

There's a murder in the art gallery, a dragon slayer on the loose and a nosy librarian turned sleuth.
Let the mayhem begin...

Xandie Meyers thought she'd found her place in the supernatural world when she moved to Point Muse, Maine. She even made new friends. But instead of settling into a peaceful new life, Xandie's dealing with rampaging zombie gnomes, bad luck, and now a poisoned dragon body has turned up in the art gallery. The Dragon clan is snarling for vengeance and her new friend is the prime suspect.

Xandie has no choice but to let her inner Sherlock librarian swing into action before an innocent

woman is jailed for a crime she didn't commit and
Point Muse dissolves into chaos.

Can Xandie survive long enough to navigate her
freaky new world? Or will things that go bump in the
night have her for a midnight snack?

Unlock the mayhem of *The Dastardly Dragon Killer
and the Poison Breath!*

ONE

"Who'd have thought ceramic garden gnomes craved blood?" Alexandra Meyers, a.k.a. Xandie, squealed when a nasty-looking gnome with a sharp fishing pole bared his teeth. She panted, her stomach a wibbly wobbly bowl full of jelly. Her attackers had such cute faces, with red cheeks and wide grins that hid sadistic Xandie-biting streaks a mile wide.

"Well, sweetie, there're rumors on the dark witch web about a breed of cursed gnomes." Elspeth lined up her crutch and let loose with a sharp underarm sweep. "Bonsai!" She cackled as a sneering miniature female with an apron, matching jaunty cap, and a tiny, sharp knife exploded into white dust.

"You want to talk about rumors when zombie gnomes are stalking us?" Xandie climbed up on the base of one of the lampposts lining Main Street. Her grandmother, Elspeth Harrow, had a somewhat dubious and mysterious past. Xandie had only known her for the last few months. The woman was a wildcard with a devious mind, but her aim was spot on. Her grandmother *had* sprained her ankle racing carts with the clothing optional octogenarian coven in town. So, the wild streak had its downside. Xandie winced when a gash on her ankle pulled tight with a sharp twang. Arms quivering, she adjusted her hands around the lamppost. Maybe it was time to try out for weight training. The burn in her muscles flared red hot the more she thought about letting go.

"There is always time for rumors, Xandie. You're a Harrow. It's in your blood."

"My father would argue it's Meyers blood, not Harrow," Xandie offered with a grimace. Her father hated Point Muse, his hometown. He'd grown up surrounded by the weird and wacky characters who populated the small Maine town. Then he'd met her mother, Miranda Harrow, and he'd convinced her to move to Andrews, a college town outside of Portland, three and half hours away from Point Muse. Not far enough if you asked Nicholas Meyers. He still hadn't forgiven his only daughter for moving and becoming the librarian to the supernatural Great Library of

Alexandria in Point Muse. Xandie shuffled her feet on the base of the lamppost, easing the tingling in her toes now.

"Huh, I guess my son-in-law is the expert then." Elspeth swung her crutch again, taking the head off a smiling statue with teeth filed into sharp points. "The rumors don't matter, anyway. These gnomes are from my collection."

"The mysterious Elspeth Harrow collects murderous ceramic garden ornaments?"

"Everyone has a hobby. Mine's cursed statues. Someone stole my head statue. Went out this morning and she was missing, and the rest only listen to her. That's why we have a bloodthirsty gaggle of gnomes here." Elspeth jabbed her crutch down on a red-capped gnome nibbling on her bandaged ankle.

Even her grandmother was spryer than she was. Taking action, Xandie swung a leg and karate-kicked a hungry milkmaid. *Score.* "Lila isn't due to open for another ten minutes and they have us pinned down. What's our next move?" *Before she fainted from excess exercise.*

"The next move is to eliminate these ornaments before they take us out, dear."

"Cursed gnomes. What else can Point Muse shock me with?" At least Theo had stayed in the library with his pet imp, Horatio. He'd wanted to practice riding techniques. Xandie's aunt, Amelia, had even made a tiny saddle for the imp. Her vet-witch aunt had proclaimed Theo, Xandie's ancient Greek-teenager-turned-cranky-black-cat-guardian, would benefit from caring for a pet. Even if the pet was a demonic denizen of Hell. Elspeth had given her stamp of approval by gifting him a tiny hot-pink tracksuit with *impish* bedazzled on the pants. Horatio loved his clothing and paraded on Theo's back, wiggling his pink tracksuit-clad bottom in pride. Since the imp had helped defend the cat from a killer knight, he'd been a fixture in the house.

"On your left," a female voice bellowed from behind Xandie.

Xandie's breathing suspended for a split second, before whooshing out in a gush as she whipped to the side to face her next attacker. The only thing she spotted was the scattered remains of her vicious ceramic stalkers. She shook her head. What the heck... "Where have they all gone?"

Elspeth still swung away at her pile of remains so where were the rest?

"Duck!"

Without thought, she dropped straight down. Crouching on the concrete base of the lamppost, she held on tight. A sword whistled overhead and a rope with ninja gnomes attached crashed to the ground in a spray of white dust. Coughing, Xandie stepped down from the lamppost and wiped her eyes. "Thanks, whoever you are. Your aim was true and noble in the slaying of blood-hungry, cursed garden ceramics."

Throat dry from the battle and the shocking ending, she licked ceramic ash from her lips. She struggled to find the words to thank her rescuer but came up short. How did you say thanks to someone who sliced rabid garden gnomes out for blood? More to the point, how did you explain the said evil doers?

"This town is a hoot. Crazy, but still a hoot. I'm Priss Makepeace, at your slaying service." A tall, athletic woman with blonde hair and a bouncy pony-tail grinned at Xandie.

"A hoot, yeah. Try saying that after those darn garden ornaments stab you in the ankle multiple times."

"Is this normal for Point Muse?"

"Eh…" Xandie rolled her eyes then smiled. "I'm Xandie Meyers. Your assist arrived just in time." Her savior towered over her own five-foot-five height, handy when you needed garden gnome slaying. Xandie loved her sugar too much to give it up in favor of exercise, especially sword related workouts, which meant she was well padded in certain areas. Unlike the slim and muscled woman in front of her.

"My pleasure. Like I said, you can use my slaying skills anytime." Priss shook the dust from her sword and glanced at Xandie's companion.

Xandie followed her gaze, concerned for Elspeth. But her grandmother had decimated her foes and cradled a snapping fishing gnome before twisting his head off.

"You good, Elspeth?" Never underestimate the upper arm strength of a reformed dark witch octogenarian.

Elspeth dusted her hands off, grabbed her crutch, and hobbled over to her granddaughter. "That's a great cardio workout. Shame about my gnomes, though." Elspeth sighed and then shot a questioning glance from amber-colored Harrow eyes at the blonde, ceramic-slaying heroine.

"Priss Makepeace, champion with a sword." Priss nodded at Elspeth and gestured with a sword-free hand. "So, is this a regular killing celebration? I arrived a few weeks ago, and everything seemed quiet then."

Elspeth narrowed her gaze. "And who are you?"

"I'm the temporary fill-in for the sports instructor

at Point Muse Academy while the current teacher is on maternity leave." Priss saluted carefully with her short sword. "I'm renting an apartment on Main Street. I was running through some sword training when I saw you being attacked. Thought I'd come and help."

"Thank God you did." Xandie kicked the rope the gnomes had climbed down and shuddered when she spotted the rough noose fashioned at the bottom.

Flipping a switch from suspicious to welcoming, Elspeth patted Priss on her sword arm. "Thanks for helping my granddaughter."

"I thought you might be related. You have the same amber-colored eyes."

"Family trait. Xandie's not used to the cutthroat world of Point Muse yet. She's a sheltered librarian."

"Hey," the sheltered librarian protested. "I've been here a couple months."

"Most of it spent in jail or running away from knightly killers or stuffing your face with Lila's butter puffs." Elspeth poked Xandie's rear end. "Add cardio to your library duties." Elspeth smirked and patted her hot-pink coiffed hairdo. "Right, I'm off to hunt down my last gnome. Some cretin stole her, and she's a cursed Sumerian demon. I need to get her back. Toodles." She waved to the other two women and hobbled off toward Harrow House.

Xandie turned to the gnome-slayer and was surprised to catch a flicker of regret on the stranger's face. "You okay? The weird that is Point Muse isn't for everyone."

Priss shook herself like a wet dog. "Weird doesn't disturb me. My father dabbled in the mystical security business while he raised me. I've seen enough to know that Point Muse is normal for a supernatural town."

"Wizard or sorcerer?" Two or three months ago, she'd never have been able to say that phrase without snorting or calling the crazy police.

"Magical security with enhanced weapons, hence the sword." Priss sheathed her weapon at her waist. "Your grandmother mentioned you're a librarian?"

Xandie snorted. Librarian didn't seem to cover her job description. "I'm the librarian, curator, and general dog's body to the library."

Eyes rounded, Priss whistled. "The Librarian, emphasis on *the*. My dad told me about the library. Guess I better stay on your good side."

"Xandie doesn't have a good side, it's all downhill from here." Lila stuck her head through her open bakery door. "Come in, brave gnome fighters. I have rich, gooey chocolate chip cookies as a reward."

Thank God for her family and chocolate. This day was looking up. Xandie followed Priss into the bakery and collapsed on a chair in relief. She waved a hand in a bustling Lila's direction. "That's my cousin, Lila Harrow. She owns this bakery, Heart's Delight, and she makes a mean hot chocolate."

The gnome slayer shuddered. "No thanks. Give me a full-bodied, saucy cappuccino any day."

"And ladies, that's why I'm the boss." Lila placed a hot chocolate next to Xandie and a cappuccino in front of Priss, who sniffed the cup with her eyes closed before she savored the first sip. Lila snickered. "Coffee lover?"

"Since I was a teenager. Whenever I competed, I had an early start. Coffee was the only stimulant that kept me awake."

"I figure since you're carrying that pig sticker, it must mean you fence?" Lila nodded at the sword strapped to the other woman's hip.

"My dad taught me. I don't compete anymore, but I'm instructing at the academy."

Xandie snorted. "Good luck on getting any of those kids to care. From what I've noticed, supernatural kids are spoiled as hell."

Priss grimaced. "I'm finding that out, but I haven't been here long though. I thought I'd try something different after my father died. Point Muse offered me a paying position. So, here I am." She stared down at her almost empty cappuccino.

Lila bounced up as the first of the morning trade trickled in. "Well, we're glad to have you. Especially Xandie, since you saved her from death by garden ornament."

"Funny, Lila. Real funny." Since solving her great-aunt's murder and her mother's disappearance, Xandie had settled into the chaos of Harrow family life.

"I can see the family resemblance between all of you. The eyes and the same shade of brown hair. I take it you're close to your cousin?"

"There are three of us cousins, the same age. I've only known Lila and Holly for a few months, though. But it feels like I've gained two annoying sisters."

"I can hear you," Lila sang from behind the counter. She yelled over her shoulder for help, and a grim-faced teenage girl with black and silver hair stomped out.

Xandie whispered to Priss. "Work experience. Es wanted to work with my other cousin, Holly, at the funeral home, but the school wouldn't okay it. So, she's stuck with Lila. Can anyone say dragon with attitude?"

"She's a dragon?" Priss dropped her hand to her sword. Knuckles white, she turned her torso away from the teenager, shielding herself.

Wow, Priss looked like she'd sucked on a lemon. "Es Penne. She's not too painful as teenagers or dragons go. The rest of the clan is snooty Point Muse high society." At least the dragons had backed off once she'd tracked down the killer knight who'd murdered several Point Muse residents. But they still hadn't warmed to Xandie as librarian.

"My dad always said a good dragon was a quiet one. He meant dead, not silent, but in his mind, it still applied." Priss threw money on the table and shot Xandie a lukewarm smile. "I have to finish sword practice, but thanks for the coffee. I'll see you sometime." Priss waved as she strode out the door.

Lila wandered over and dumped a plate of Xandie's favorite sweets, golden honey butter puffs, in front of her. "Did my coffee drive our new resident away?"

Xandie frowned. "She left pretty abruptly. As soon as she found out Es was a dragon, she dropped this weird comment about dead dragons and left."

Xandie grabbed a puff and nibbled, contemplating Priss Makepeace. She chewed and waited for the smooth sweetness overload but was met with the slagging taste of pure bitter salt. Xandie spat her puff out and gulped her hot chocolate.

Lila reared back, horrified. "What's wrong? Butter puffs are your favorite."

"I'm sorry, but it tasted bitter. I think you used salt instead of sugar."

"That's not possible. I know this recipe by heart. I know I used sugar." Lila pushed her chair away and stood, looking wildly around the bakery.

People hunched over their plates, spitting out food left and right. Table after table had the same reaction. Customers stood, shouting at Lila and Es as they tried to calm them down. People even shoved each other.

Xandie waded in to deal with the irate customers. She couldn't help but think rampaging garden gnomes, spoiled food, and a mysterious new resident weren't the best portents for a calm, trouble-free Point Muse.

TWO

"My regulars hate me." Lila hung her head in her hands.

"They don't hate you. Although those women you hosed down might harbor ill will." Xandie gaped at the chaos surrounding her. A tornado of furious customers had whirled through Lila's beloved bakery. Overturned tables, food splattered everywhere. Plates broken into tiny pieces covered the floor like a crazed ceramic obstacle course.

"I don't get it. Heart's Delight is just that. I don't do potions or spells, hexes, or curses, like Elspeth used to. My witchiness goes into my cooking. The food's supposed to enhance your mood, your confidence, help you focus on what's good in your life and in yourself. Clarity of heart, mind, and soul. That's it. Instead, my customers tried to kill each other with coffee cups." Lila groaned and lowered her head until her forehead landed with a thud on the last remaining upright table.

"Like the killer garden ornaments, something isn't right in Point Muse." Xandie patted Lila on her food-coated head.

"The brownie quit before the fight."

Lila and Xandie turned and stared at the moody dragon teenager on work experience.

Lila frowned "No way. Hannah's been with me since I opened. She's always worked for the Harrow family."

Es shrugged. "Just telling you what happened. She told me all the bad luck floating around town was looking for victims and she wasn't giving it a warm body to work with."

"Bad luck is a thing here?" *Go figure.* Point Muse never failed to surprise Xandie. She righted a couple of chairs before collapsing into one.

"The fishermen at the harbor have an ancient lantern blessed by the Greek god, Poseidon, to bring light and luck to seafarers and the town they come from. Went missing yesterday." Es dropped her verbal bombshell and kept picking chairs up.

"It's bad luck?" Lila jumped up and used

Xandie's head as a set of drums. "I knew it wasn't me."

"Elspeth has her cursed garden gnome stolen and then it's a ceramic apocalypse. The town's good luck charm is stolen, and you get spoiled food and cranky customers. This is about a thief stealing magical stuff from the town's residents?" At least it wasn't a murder this time. Finding a thief had to be easier than a murderer.

"No. Absolutely not. I know what you're thinking." Lila crossed her arms. "Last time almost ended up with you skewered by a psychotic killer knight. Leave it to law enforcement."

"Police Chief Braun's away in Portland on a course with the paranormal investigator branch. The twins are in charge. Why not help them?" Wouldn't hurt to shore up good feelings from the town as she was still on probation as librarian. And it would prove to the dragons once and for all she was the librarian.

"You mean, their mom, Agatha, is in charge." Lila snickered, her previous devastation over her subpar cooking skills all but forgotten.

Xandie stood and paced to the big picture window. From here, she had a bird's-eye view of Main Street. People gathered in small groups, hunkered together. Others rushed along the street, single-minded about their destination in an effort to outpace the rotten luck floating in the air.

"There was a fender bender when I came in this morning," Es offered and then shuddered. "The garbage truck collided with the latest catch from the harbor. Garbage and fish are not the most inspiring scent of the day."

A customer from Here Today, Gone Tomorrow, the local hairdressing salon, ran out screeching, pawing at his smoking, neon-green beehive hair. A group of people surged out of the local grocery store, swatting at a swarm of flies trailing behind them.

"It's the magical apocalypse, isn't it?" Lila joined them at the window. All three girls peered out, wondering what the next calamity would be.

"No offense, but if it rains amphibians, I'm outta here. Work experience or not." The teenager flicked at her white-streaked black hair and glowered.

Xandie snapped her fingers. "Hey, I met the academy's newest teacher this morning. She even came with her own sword." Priss had rushed to her rescue and seemed lovely, until the dragon had entered the picture. Then she'd turned weird.

"Ms. Makepeace." Es rolled her kohl-rimmed eyes. "She's okay, doesn't like me much. And she has way too much of an unhealthy attachment to her sword. Dragons don't have the best relationships with sharp and pointy, unless it's their own teeth." She bared her pearly whites and, with a sharkish smile, sauntered off to right more chairs.

"No offense, but dragon teenagers are worse than hormonal humans."

Lila nodded. "No argument there. What's the next step, Nancy Drew?"

Xandie opened the door and scanned the street. "I risk life and limb to visit the police. See what Aggie knows about missing artifacts."

"Don't forget to check on your furry sidekick, and the library might have an idea about what's going on." Lila grabbed a broom and swept the food-covered floor.

Waving goodbye, Xandie stepped out onto the street and headed for the police station run by the bear-shifting Braun family. Taking a side street, she passed the Point Muse gallery and antique store. Iris Malone, the owner, had a mix of paintings, photos, sculptures, and all manner of antiques and decorative arts. At least, that's what the promotional flyer shoved in her mailbox stated.

An empty alley ran between the gallery and an old diner. Residents used it as a shortcut to the other side of town. As Xandie turned into the alley, voices caught her attention. For some reason, the raised timbre in the voices had her heart thumping. Fight or flight reflex engaged, as did her self-preservation. One thing finding dead bodies had taught her was everyone had secrets. Sometimes it was just better in the long run if one kept a safe distance and eavesdropped like heck. Ducking behind a low brick wall, she strained to hear.

"I'm out. Do you understand me?" A male voice rumbled over a fainter female one.

"You're out when I say you are. *You* approached me with this plan. Remember?"

"I don't need you anymore. I have a new contact. So, I'm out." The man stomped away from the cursing woman.

Xandie ducked behind the low brick wall as Archibald Penne stormed past. Es Penne's older cousin, scribe to the keeper of the family history.

"I'm not done with you, Penne. Do you hear me?" Iris Malone screeched at Archibald, all pretense of secrecy gone in the face of her anger. "I'll make you pay if you cross me. Permanently. You hear me?" With a primal howl, she ran into the gallery, letting the door slam shut with a decisive bang.

Straightening, Xandie hoofed it to the police

station. "Now, wasn't that an interesting chat?" she mumbled, trying to puzzle out the fight she'd witnessed. Iris and Archibald were involved in something underhanded, otherwise why meet in secret? But was it the stolen magical artifacts or something else?

"If you're after Aggie, I wouldn't go inside yet." Melody Braun sat on the steps, painting her nails.

"Why? What's up?" Xandie slipped down next to the chief of police's younger sister.

"The esteemed residents of our freakish town aren't happy with the current trend of missing magical artifacts."

"Who is? Lila's baked goods turned nasty, and evil gnomes nibbled my ankles. I'm not happy either."

"What's the library say?"

"That's my next stop." Xandie shuffled her bottom on the hard step. Summer had only registered a blip on Point Muse's weather radar. A few weeks of short sleeves and now the town was back to jeans and long sleeves. "Do the twins have any ideas about the thefts?"

Melody snorted. Her wide shifter shoulders shook as she suppressed her snickers. "Ah, Zach's away and the twins have no clue. Mom isn't happy either, our great—however many—great-grandfather's pelt from the Black Forest has disappeared."

Xandie grimaced. "Why have a family member hanging on the wall?"

Melody waved a hand, drying her polish. "He was the first bear shifter in the family. Since he died, the family keeps the pelt to remind us."

"Of?"

"Never trust Goldilocks." Melody stood and capped her polish bottle. "Mom got a tip not too long ago. Told us to look at the dragons."

"Seriously? You want to tangle with dragons?"

"Hell no, not me. Who knows about my idiot brothers, though? I think we need more evidence before we look in their direction. But I thought you might be interested." Melody winked and strode inside.

A cacophony of noise, multiple voices arguing over each other, assaulted Xandie's ears. "Maybe not going in is a good idea." Getting an answer from the library might be.

Xandie headed to Lila's for a ride home. Standing on the side of the road, she looked up and down. Who knew what crazies lurked? All quiet, Xandie crossed the street. Almost at Lila's door, she spotted the new mysterious resident, talking animatedly to Archibald Penne.

"What is it about Archibald today?" She watched Priss shove a wad of papers at Archibald's chest and storm off. The dragon waited for a moment before shuffling away. "Curious and curiouser, as my late Great-Aunt Sera would say." It seemed little Priss Makepeace was a tad more involved in the town's goings-on than she'd let on. "Time for the library," Xandie murmured.

"Look what the imp dragged in." Theophilus, a.k.a. ancient Greek turned cat guardian, fluffed his fur. Raising his whiskered face into the air, he stalked past, only pausing as Horatio, his pet imp, jumped down from Xandie's shoulder and settled into the saddle on his back.

Xandie slammed her solid wood front door closed and peered around the entranceway. Polished floors and a sweeping staircase met her gaze, but no killer garden gnomes. She walked into the lounge, collapsed onto a couch, and crossed her arms. "Don't push me. I've taken down killer ceramics, and I can handle a mouthy feline."

Theo coughed a hairball next to Xandie's feet as Horatio adjusted his saddle. "Please, don't make me throw up on your pillow again. All I'm saying is you left this morning to help that nightmare of a grandmother, and it's almost lunch. Horatio and I could have starved waiting for you to come home."

"You're an ancient Greek teenager turned into a feline guardian. How hard can it be to get your own food?" She glared at Theo with a fixed stare. She'd fought off ankle savages and he wanted feeding? The cat needed priorities.

"Hard with no hands." He flashed claws and took a swipe at her ankles. He paused mid swing when he noticed the red scratches already decorating the skin there. "What gives? You got another starving cat that's taken a swing at you?"

"That would be a negative, feline. A garden gnome's fishing pole and countless tiny teeth using me as a chew toy caused those marks." Xandie rubbed the cuts and heaved a sigh. Pushing herself off the couch, she limped to the kitchen and the cat chow. Best to feed the hangry complainer or she'd never hear the end of it. Theo followed behind, peppering her with questions.

She dumped cat biscuits into two bowls for Theo and his pet imp. After tracking down the rampaging killer Sanguis Knight, who'd murdered her great-aunt Sera among other victims, her cat had adopted Horatio. As far as she could tell the tiny Hell resident ate anything but loved tacos and salmon-flavored biscuits most.

"Details, Meyers. What gives with the slash marks? Are you feeling *emo,* or have you taken up with another furry supernatural entity?"

"I can barely deal with the cat I've got, let alone another." But the library might have answers on the spate of magical robberies.

"Come on, Meyers. I'll clean up that hairball in your shoe closet if you give me deets."

Xandie shuddered. Slang from a feline was just wrong, plain wrong. "Someone's stealing magical artifacts in town. They stole Elspeth's cursed demon, and bad luck is stalking the town. At least, at the moment. I need to talk to the library about it."

"Wow, killer gnomes. How Point Muse." Theo trotted into the library and jumped on the desk with the appointment book. Horatio squealed and held a hand high, like a rodeo rider.

Xandie had cleared all her requests before she visited Lila, and nothing else was pending. She grabbed hold of her necklace shaped like a triangle with an eye in its center and focused her question. "Who's stealing from Point Muse?"

"You don't need to hold the necklace; the library knows what you want. Besides, if it ain't supernatural, it can't help."

"What are the odds the theft of magical artifacts is a run-of-the-mill normal human crime?" Xandie raised an eyebrow.

The library eased a book out of one of the shelves until it fell to the floor. Xandie smiled victoriously at Theo and snatched it up. "Treaties on draconic movement. How does that help us?"

"Well..." He dragged out the word. "We have a dragon family in Point Muse. Maybe it concerns them?"

She scanned the contents and skipped to the Penne chapter. "The Pendrakons are European dragons who settled in the eighteen hundreds in Point Muse, Maine. A magical, supernatural community settled on ley lines. The clan is matriarchal, and the current head is Marjorie Penne. Her heir is Adelind Penne. Previous heir, Melinda Penne, disappeared without a trace, along with her mate, a dragon slayer."

Xandie turned the problem over in her mind. "Priss froze and left the bakery when she spotted Es

Penne. Plus, she told me her father always said a good dragon was a dead one." Was Priss related to them? "Or is the matriarch thieving magical objects to build up her horde?" Xandie snickered. "I can't see uptight, snooty Marjorie Penne stealing artifacts, can you?"

"They're dragons who hoard treasure. Who knows?" He started to groom the imp, much to Horatio's dismay. Shrill squeaking from the imp and the shaking of tiny fists drove Xandie from her reading chair. She pushed the book back into place on the shelf. She might need it later.

Sometimes the library worked in obscure ways; it was up to the librarian to decipher the message and how it related to her question.

She hoped she was up to the job.

THREE

"A few days of peace. That's all I wanted. Instead, I've had five days of pain and suffering." Xandie let her head sag into her hands, exhaustion in every line of her body.

"Never mind. Maybe a nice murder will pop up soon. Take your mind off the rampaging mob storming the library if you don't find the missing artifacts." Holly snickered to herself.

"Way to bring her down, death girl." Lila shoved a block of dark chocolate at Xandie. "Quick, consume it before the damn thing turns into a salt block or before Aunt Winifred sees it."

Grabbing a chunk of chocolate, Xandie munched it down. Most of the Harrow women had a sweet tooth. They were sitting in Harrow House; odds were the block wouldn't last long. "Thanks," she mumbled around a mouthful of chocolate.

"Eh." Lila shrugged. "Not my house, not my chocolate. I stole it from Holly's stash."

Holly rolled her eyes. "That's not my real stash. It's the cheap stuff to fool those who filch my stash."

"Still good." Xandie swallowed her sugary treat and leaned against the burgundy velvet couch. Harrow House was an old Victorian; it had held the family of witches since the town settled. Now, only Elspeth, Winifred, and Holly lived here. Old photos decorated the walls and fought for space with childish drawings from years ago. The furniture had a lived-in and loved-hard look, but it suited the house and her family. The crazy, eclectic Harrows, her mother's family. Happy, warm earth witches, all except Elspeth, the matriarch of the clan, who refused to discuss her past or her powers except for the odd shocking tidbit. *Speak of the witch...*

"Aha, look what the witch found." Elspeth sashayed in, beaming from ear to ear. She shoved her prize up in the air like a trophy. A squat, horned, wrinkled ceramic trophy.

"Geez, please don't tell me you're collecting gnomes again?" Xandie pushed herself back into the couch and covered her ankles. The great garden ornament slaughter may have been a week ago, but her ankles still ached. She was a gnome no-go zone.

Elspeth coughed. "Please, this is my one and only cursed Sumerian demon. Found her on the doorstep when I came home from the hairdresser." She cradled her ceramic gnome and rubbed the horns. "Who's my sweet evil goddess? You are." She cackled as the lights flickered off and on.

"Gran, you're giving off the evil witch vibe again. Besides, when did the hairdressing salon open? I thought the shop closed because of the flammable hair product incident?"

Elspeth twitched her lilac bobbed wig into place with one hand. "They aren't taking on clients yet, but they are offering deals on wigs. This baby was a steal."

Xandie raised her morose face. "Bad luck still hanging around town and you buy a wig?" She yawned and fought the urge to lean back in the couch and catch a snooze. Every waking moment at home was spent puzzling the mystery of the magical artifacts, so sleep had become optional. She was too worried someone would petition the library for her removal because of her inability to solve a puzzle. That and the fact Horatio the imp snored like an elephant roaring. Who'd have thought someone so little could churn out a foghorn?

"You make your fun where you can, sweet Alexandra. Besides, the electric tension is fantastic for my complexion." Elspeth cackled again and danced with her Sumerian garden gnome underarm.

"Watch out, Mother, you're flashing your inner evil. Best cover up." Winifred sailed into Harrow House with an arm full of thick creamy candles. She placed them around the room and dusted off her hands.

"Ah, Mom? Don't you think we have enough candles already? You haven't worn through the first hundred in the house yet?" Holly glared at her plump and way-too-cheerful mother.

"One can never have enough candles if you're a witch." Winifred clapped her hands, and every candle flickered to life. "Now, Xandie, this is for you. To offer clarity of mind and soul to help you fix the problem Point Muse is having."

"No offense, Aunt Win, but how do candles help me?"

"Candle magic gathers the powers of fire and initiates change. Fire transforms and purifies the mind and the body and the spirit." Winifred frowned at the group of Harrow women arranged on the couch. "I used the last of my dragon resin to make these virgin candles, so pay attention."

"Long time since virgin anything lived in this house." Lila winked.

Xandie and Holly fought the giggles while Elspeth gave into grating hyena brays of laughter.

"You knew using virgin would screw with them. How can they take you seriously?" Lila's mother, Amelia, lounged against the wall to the kitchen.

Xandie's Aunt Amelia was the polar opposite to her younger sister. Tall and skinny with an athletic build but with the same amber Harrow eyes all the women, including Xandie, had.

"Well, maybe grown women should be mature, well-adjusted adults, instead of giggling ninnies," Winifred snapped.

"Speak for yourself. How I raised such strait-laced daughters is beyond me. Must be your father's influence." Elspeth sniffed and shoved her gnome under a canary yellow pants-suited arm. "Excuse me, I'm off to suck up the excess tension." She stomped off and left the room.

"Well, looks like her ankle is better." Amelia lowered herself into a fluffy armchair.

"She probably sucked the life out of a virgin and used it to heal herself." Lila waggled her eyebrows at her cousins and set them giggling again.

"Lila Harrow! That's your grandmother. We never admit she can suck the life out of someone." Amelia glared at her unrepentant daughter.

"If the evil witch hat fits." Lila shrugged.

"Can we please focus on my candles?" Winifred sighed. "Center your thoughts. Have a question paramount in your mind and repeat after me…"

Xandie tried to clear her mind. But the picture of Elspeth sucking the soul out of a virgin was hard to forget.

Winifred continued, "Clarity, clarity, come to me. Mind, body, and soul must see. With this spell, the fog disappears. This is my will. So mote it be." She looked expectantly at her niece.

Xandie searched for answers to Point Muse's thieving issues but came up blank. "Sorry, Aunt Winifred. I got nothing." She pinched her lips together and then took a deep breath. Winifred was helping her, and still she had nothing. No answers as to what scheme the thief played out. She'd thought after solving a murder, a series of magical robberies would be as easy as eating Lila's butter puffs. *Apparently not.*

Waving a hand, Winifred snuffed all the candles

out in the house. "It was worth a try. Maybe the question needs longer to percolate in your soul before you get an answer?"

"She's not a coffee machine, Aunt Win." Lila stood and pulled Xandie and Holly up. "We have to get going anyway. The gallery has a special showing tonight of dragon hoard artifacts from the Penne collection, and I'm catering. I have to deliver my non-salty goodies to Iris Malone."

"Fine, whatever." Winifred gathered her candles and stomped away, as irritated as an annoying optimist could be.

The girls gathered at the front door of Harrow House and slipped their jackets on.

"Psst, Xandie." Elspeth stood at the top of the stairs and gestured her up.

Telling her cousins to wait outside, Xandie clambered up the stairs to Elspeth. "Everything okay, G?" Xandie couldn't bring herself to call the active, kooky, and sometimes mysterious woman in front of her Grandmother. G or Elspeth fit much better.

"Oh, everything's a hoot." Elspeth grinned malevolently, then sobered as she peered at Xandie. "Your mother wasn't the strongest witch, and she never found her special groove the way the other two have. But she was always a catalyst and brought things to a conclusion. You have that same quality. Don't let those clingy Point Muse harpies get you down. You'll work things out."

"Thanks, Elspeth. I hope you're right."

"And if you're lucky, you'll find another body. That'll shake up the town and get their mind off their troubles." She slapped Xandie on the shoulder and cackled evil-hag style before slipping off to her room with a slam of the door.

"Why does everyone want me to find another body?" Xandie mumbled to herself as she joined her cousins outside.

Anyone would think bodies followed her.

"It's full-bodied, with great potential for elemental satisfaction." The smarmy art critic gushed over a curved pitted dragon tooth on display. "My family donated this precious artifact and others in the collection in the hopes other supernatural families could share in our unique lifestyle. A red dot means the artifact is for sale." Ronald Penne adjusted his silk tie and searched for someone in the crowd before disappearing over to another popular artifact to spin his sales talk again.

"Pompous art talk for it's a big tooth so buy, buy, buy," Xandie whispered to Holly, who scowled at her.

"Shush, I like dragon teeth. Ronald Penne is right, some of these artifacts are fascinating."

"Isn't that morbid? The fang must have belonged to someone. And I can't see a dragon volunteering a tooth. Especially not such a slick salesman as Mr. Penne."

"Please, Xandie. I work in a funeral home and have visions of people dying sometimes. Morbid doesn't worry me."

Xandie nibbled on an appetizer and considered Holly. She'd worked at the funeral home for a while. But her cousin seemed stressed and snappy. Holly was the quiet Harrow who held Lila's foot-and-mouth leash. "What's up, Holly? You seem kind of on edge."

Giving into hunger, Holly shoveled three cheese cubes into her mouth and mumbled around them. Swallowing, she repeated her words, "I thought working at Elysian Fields would be a good way to get a handle on my banshee gifts. Plus, with the necromancer twins who own the home, I thought it might help."

"But?"

"But my visions are on the fritz." Holly sighed and snatched an orange juice from a passing server. "My father thinks it's the Harrow blood and the Maguire banshee blood battling each other. I have to wait and see who wins." She wrinkled her nose and pouted.

"I guess it makes sense. Your mom and dad don't know how your gifts will interact. Just be patient. I'm sure you'll see someone die soon." Xandie poked her tongue out at her cousin.

"Put that away. Who knows where it's been?" Lila moved behind Xandie and Holly and gathered up empty trays.

"It's been eating your cheese cubes."

"Oh, poor baby. Sheriff hot-pants Braun isn't here, and Xandie's lonely and grumpy."

Xandie choked on a cheese cube. "For your information, Lila Harrow, Sheriff Braun arrested me. I have no interest in his pants, hot or otherwise."

"Saying it aloud doesn't make it so, oh great librarian."

Ignoring her cousin's teasing, Xandie glared at the art crowd milling around. Half a dozen dragon artifacts from claws, fangs, and scales to ancient books, jewelry, and tapestries, hung on display. Ronald Penne, mate to the Penne heir, mingled with the elite of Point Muse while projecting a fake air of social goodwill to convince people to buy his dragon art.

"Looks like Iris got a good crowd." Lila leaned over Holly and snatched a platter of appetizers out of her hand. "Your waistline doesn't need those."

Holly crammed another cheese cube into her mouth and ignored Lila.

"It helps that nothing weird has happened the last forty-eight hours."

Xandie let out a little shriek as Priss Makepeace popped up next to her.

Orange juice swamped the side of Xandie's glass as her hands shook at the sudden interruption. She turned and carefully placed it on the table behind her. "Are you in stealth mode?"

Priss stared at her champagne and then back to Xandie. "No, more alcoholic mode." She raised a glass in salute to Lila's catering.

"Are you an art appreciator?" Holly joined the conversation as Lila cleaned behind them.

She shrugged. "Sometimes. I'm more into swords, but dragon artifacts can be interesting. I hear that Archibald Penne from the Penne clan helped supply the artifacts. You see him anywhere?"

Hadn't Priss argued with Archibald just five days ago? Why was she searching him out now? "I wouldn't have thought dragons were your thing. Didn't you tell me your father preferred a dead dragon to a talkative one?" Xandie's pulse raced; having some of her questions answered would go a long way toward shutting up the gossips and ending their pressure to solve the thefts. Not to mention cementing her reputation as the librarian. And the mysterious sword wielder was beginning to appear shadier by the minute.

Priss bared her teeth in a close copy of a smile. "His actual words were the only good dragon was a quiet dragon. But whatever. Doesn't mean I agree with everything he said." She looked sad for a moment.

Talk about the guilts. Xandie felt like a bully. "Sorry, I must've misunderstood. Ignore me." Xandie offered an apologetic smile.

"No problem. Death and dads are touchy subjects."

"Dead mothers too."

Holly butted in between the two girls. "And absent fathers."

A cackle sounded from the corner, and all three women turned and watched Elspeth shimmy across the floor in a lime-green pantsuit with a bowl of fruit on her head.

"Grandmothers too," chorused Holly and Xandie.

Priss snorted into her champagne glass and sloshed her top with alcohol. "Well, I have to say your family isn't boring." She placed her glass down. "I think I'll mop this up." She indicated her champagne-sprinkled top and waggled her fingers in a goodbye. Priss headed off, perky blonde ringlets bouncing.

"That girl confuses me. One moment, grim and focused, the next, cheerleader. It's exhausting." Xandie puzzled over the mystery of Priss Makepeace. She liked the fencing instructor, but something about the woman niggled at her.

"Cheer up. No glum faces at the Iris Malone Gallery." Iris Malone walked toward Xandie and handed her another orange juice. "In fact, you know what cheers me up? Buying art. The pieces here tonight have been donated by Ronald Penne and the Penne clan."

"Not on a librarian's wage."

"Or a funeral assistant's. We're just here to support Lila," Holly offered.

Iris waved the words way. "One can always appreciate art, even if they can't afford it."

"Are all the pieces from the Penne dragon hoard?" Xandie asked Iris, still feeling guilty for eating and not buying anything.

"Oh, yes. The Penne clan is very generous. Not everything's for sale, but Ronald Penne has marked the descriptions in the catalogue. Archibald worked with Ronald and me to produce a top-notch collection."

The same Archibald Penne Xandie had seen arguing with both Priss and Iris only five days ago. "Is he here tonight?"

Iris smiled over Xandie's shoulder at another potential customer. "He's here somewhere, as is his Uncle Ronald. Can't have a gallery showing of dragon artifacts without a few in residence. God knows, Marjorie or her heir, Adelind, wouldn't get caught dead here. Ronald performs most of the social duties for the clan. Now, I must move on. Enjoy the art." Iris floated away and buttonholed another art goer.

"That woman smiles too much," Holly grumbled. "It's like talking to a shark. I guess it's natural. Her mother's a dwarf, and they're all about gold and acquisition."

Xandie set her juice on the table. "You know what? I've had my fill of the Point Muse social circle. You want to leave?"

"Thank God. I thought you'd never ask." Holly grabbed the last cheese cube and munched.

"Right, you stay here. I'll let Lila know we're going." Xandie threaded her way through the crowd until she reached the back of the gallery. The *employee only* doors were ajar. Xandie shuffled a few steps into the hallway and called Lila's name. No one replied, but a figure at the end of the corridor ducked out of the exit.

"If that's you, Lila, you're too old to play hide and seek." She cracked a smile at the thought of her cousin hiding behind some old statue. Following the figure, she eased open the exit door and scanned the alley, but it was clear. Confused, Xandie turned when she heard the thump of something hitting the floor. Her heart pounded in her chest as she moved in the direction the noise had come from and entered a galley-sized kitchen.

Chills cascaded down her spine when she spied Archibald Penne on the floor, his body twisted like a pretzel, his face an odious silvery-green, and his tongue protruding. A wisp of smoke trickled out of his open mouth. "Oh, my God." Xandie froze, hands over her mouth.

"It wasn't me. I swear. Believe me." Priss Makepeace stepped over Archibald's body, hand outstretched. In the other hand, she held a crystal vial of smoking green liquid.

Point Muse. Always a surprise and a body count…

FOUR

"I swear I didn't kill Penne." Priss smoothed her wrinkled shirt over her jeans. The same outfit she'd worn last night to the exhibition when Xandie had discovered her with Archibald Penne's dead body.

Xandie evaluated Priss and her appearance. Sure, she was rumpled—the woman had spent a night in the Point Muse lock-up—but she didn't seem satisfied or pleased with her deadly handiwork. If anything, her pacing, the clenched jaw, and her pinched lips indicated frustration, not guilt. So why did Xandie feel as if the woman hid a mile-wide secret from her?

"I found you standing over his corpse with a poison bottle in your hand." Xandie rubbed her aching head. She'd sent Holly for Agatha as soon as she found Archibald. The Brauns stepped in, removed Priss for questioning, and closed the gallery. The police chief was away, of course. Otherwise, she'd never be allowed to quiz a potential murderer. "Why were you standing over him with the poison?"

"Argh." The incarcerated woman threw up her hands and paced the cell. "We had a meeting. I found him dead. That's it."

"Why meet with him? No offense, but you don't like dragons much, do you?" Xandie asked Priss in a flat tone. She'd seen the dragon victim arguing with both Priss and the gallery owner. Why the sudden popularity with the town's female residents?

Priss nibbled her lip, her cheerleader blonde locks limp and non-bouncy. "The meeting was personal. But I didn't kill him. That's all anyone needs to know." She pounded a fist against the wall, then slumped onto a bench.

Xandie fought the swell of compassion threatening to swamp her logic centers. Sighing, she waved at Agatha to let her out. "When you're ready to tell the truth, get Agatha to call me. I like you. You saved me from killer garden ornaments, but I can't help you unless you let me." She waited until Agatha let her out and paused, staring at the murder suspect. A disheveled, scared, and mysterious Priss Makepeace.

It was time to bring the girls in and Nancy Drew the heck out of Archibald's murder. Xandie stepped out of the station and raised her face to the sun peeking through the gray clouds. Another murder to solve.

Wait until Theo hears.

"Our little sword wielder is a killer? *Cool.*" Lila drifted around the library, trailing fingers over wooden shelves.

"Are you checking out Xandie's housekeeping?" Holly griped at Lila.

"Well, it'd be nice if someone cleaned my apartment once in a while."

"How about the owner of said apartment?" Holly shot back.

"How about the freeloader who stays because she can't stand living with her mother?"

"Stop squabbling over my lack of dust. The library handles it. Can we get back on target?" Xandie rolled her eyes. Her cousins fought over anything, given the chance.

"Fine." Lila flounced to the same couch Holly lounged on and perched on the edge with a frown.

"Yeah. You guys will solve this murder. No

worries for the woman on potential death row." Theo the fluffy black cat, a.k.a. ancient Greek teenager, strolled around the room. Horatio hung off his ear, free climbing Theo's face.

"Hey," Xandie protested. "I've solved multiple murders."

"You were lucky and don't forget we all rode to your rescue." Theo made his point by flinging up his head. Horatio squealed as he flew into the air. Theo sighed and shot his paw out, flicking Horatio onto his back. Protesting, the imp crawled into his handmade saddle and adjusted his pink-spangled jogging suit.

"I had it in hand. Now we focus on Priss. Remember her? Languishing in jail for a crime she didn't commit?"

Holly held up a hand. "Are we positive she isn't guilty? I mean she's nice and has a cool sword. But we don't know her."

"I hate to agree with my death-obsessed cousin. What *do* we know of Priss Makepeace? Is that even her name?" Lila said.

"Okay, she's sketchy, and she argued with Archibald, but Malone threatened him too." Xandie flashed to Priss's reaction to Es Penne, Lila's newest work experience girl. "I have unanswered questions for her. But murder is a big stretch."

"I suggest you find background on murder girl, Iris Malone, and how the dragon died. You have a week before the Chief comes back from his course. After that, you won't get a look in." Theo galloped past with Horatio heehawing on his back.

Lila rose. "It's a plan. What does the library say?"

Xandie opened the volume on dragon migrations. She showed it to her cousins. "But what it has to do with the missing artifacts, I've no clue."

"Go through it. See what sparks that suspicious sleuthing mind of yours. Meanwhile, we'll find out what killed Archibald. Meet up with you later." Lila dragged Holly up, and they left, still squabbling.

Xandie dropped the book and took hold of her necklace. The pendant belonged to her great-aunt, Sera, the previous librarian. The necklace, library, and Theo were her inheritance. She smoothed a finger over the design. The pendant represented the symbol of knowledge. Originally, it had been a focal link between her and the library. But she'd found out when a killer knight attacked her that she could communicate with the library without it. But she felt a connection to her murdered great-aunt when she wore it. For now, she still used the necklace to help focus her questions. Xandie had already asked about the artifact thefts. So, this time, she formed her question differently. "Someone killed Archibald Penne. Is the killer a supernatural?"

The tome on draconic movement shivered and shook again. "Okay, I get the message." She patted her desk and whispered a thank you. Didn't hurt to play nice with the supernatural entity that controlled her paycheck. She dropped to the couch vacated by her warring cousins.

Xandie resigned herself to reading. She scanned the contents and turned to the Pendrakon chapter. She skipped past the information she'd read earlier. "Point Muse is a favorite of otherworldly creatures. It's a supernatural, relatively isolated community, built on a nexus of ley lines. Visitors access the town from off the highway. A lake borders one side, with a forested reserve on the other. The secluded area has an abundant national park, hiking trails, and a bustling harbor and fishing trade. Great background, but what about the Penne family?"

With no answer forthcoming, she sighed and went back to her reading. "The clan's matriarch is Marjorie. Previous heir was Melinda, who left with a mate of questionable origins. Current heir is Adelind, mate Ronald, and one female offspring." Female offspring was Es, moody teenager. Xandie mentally fussed over the problem. "Priss froze at the bakery when she spotted the teenager. Plus, she'd said her father always told her a good dragon was a dead dragon." Did Priss have an inherited grudge against dragons?

"Doesn't clear her name. It adds more questions." She needed details, and murder girl wasn't divulging any tidbits. Still thinking things through, Xandie bustled around, cleaning and adjusting books on shelves. She checked the appointment book for any requests. Then she raced through the pile of notes, writing appointments and copying information. Books and scrolls jiggled and bounced on the shelves as an industrious Xandie cleared her desk.

Reaching the final note, she read it twice before speaking. "Seriously? You couldn't have brought this to my attention earlier?" The lights overhead flickered furiously. "Sorry, sorry." She held a hand up. "My bad." She turned her attention to the note. "Archibald Penne requests an updated report on his family tree." Why investigate your own family tree? "Unless someone had new information and he'd wanted to verify it before going to the old battleax, Marjorie Penne." Archibald had argued with both women. But Priss had a sword *and* a father who hated dragons. Xandie had a sudden idea about what her new friend hid.

Sliding the request between two pages in the dragon text, she re-shelved it. She still needed more concrete material evidence.

But first task—tackle hormonal supernatural teenagers and the exhausted staff of the academy. Priss had a job there. Surely, the school had a record of her details? Now all Xandie had to do was figure out how she could acquire it.

Point Muse. Never dull.

FIVE

"Point Muse Academy, the red brick educational black hole, where hormonal mini adults go to stagnate," Es Penne intoned in a macabre voice-over as she gave Xandie a tour of the school.

Was it luck or fate when the office picked the dragon for the tour? "I take it you're not a fan of the academy?"

Es hunched her shoulders and toyed with a silver-streaked lock of black hair. "It's okay. At least I'm away from the parents."

"Moody teen with parents who don't understand, a teenage cliché." Xandie hadn't realized she'd spoken the words aloud until Es snickered.

"Mostly, I stay with my grandmother. Can't stand my parents sniping at each other or my dad's social sucking up. He'd do anything to be the center of society."

"My father's the same, except in Andrews, and he's a human librarian, not a dragon." Maybe she'd underestimated the sulky teen. Es had her own valid reasons to not care. "Is your grandmother hard to live with? I heard she could be difficult."

Es burst into a full belly laugh. Wiping her eyes, she took a deep breath and paused at the open gym doors. "Yeah, she's got a rep for being cranky, but we get on well. The old girl's got life in her yet, and she doesn't care about other people's opinions." Es waved Xandie into the gym. "This is the academy's pride and joy. My father donated the money for it. Aren't I a special snowflake?"

Xandie stared. Nothing like this in Andrews where she'd gone to school. A large gymnasium, complete with three full-size basketball courts, an indoor track, wrestling facility, and a fencing room were on offer. The students even had access to strength training equipment and cardio machines.

"Over the top. That's Ronald Penne for you."

"If he's your father, shouldn't he have a different name?"

Es led Xandie over to the fencing room. "Not if you're from a socially non-existent family and get the

Penne heir pregnant. Then you drop your own name and become a fake Penne. Told you, my dad's about social climbing."

Didn't sound as if Es liked good old dad much. Xandie wondered what Adelind, her mom, was like. She'd spotted Ronald at the gallery on the night of Archibald's murder, but the heir hadn't appeared. Xandie stepped into the fencing room, Priss Makepeace's current working space. "So, Ms. Makepeace is filling in for your old fencing instructor?"

Es leaned against a wall. "Yeah, for the last few weeks. Not much longer though, I guess."

"Because of your cousin's murder?"

"Archibald's okay, but he was like my father. Always looking for a way up and a quick buck. I'm not surprised someone took him out, just that it was Ms. Makepeace."

"Why? You don't think she could kill anyone?"

The teenager's answer interested Xandie, since Priss hated dragons so much.

"Oh, no." Es shook her head, and her choppy bangs settled back into place. "She could kill someone with that sword. You should see her train." The teenager waved at the floors. "We have thick martial arts mats and a special sprung hardwood floor that helps absorb shock. When she trains, she's focused, lethal. If she would kill anyone, it would be with a sword. I can't see her doing it with poison."

"Poison killed him? What kind?"

The dragon bit her lip and averted her eyes. "I heard a rumor, no clue if it's right. My parents won't tell me, and my grandmother doesn't want to worry me."

Dragon white lie. Xandie changed the subject. "How's Ms. Makepeace as a teacher?"

"I love the slicing and dicing with the swords. Makepeace is strict, but she doesn't play favorites. That's rare here." Es shrugged, all noncommittal teenager. "But I'm not sure she's comfortable teaching super kids. She's kinda uptight. She doesn't do much with me, but I'm used to it. Not many people like the Penne clan."

The teenager appeared to enjoy the outsider role.

"Thanks for the tour. Could you take me to the office? This campus is big enough I'll get lost." Xandie smiled at the dragon, who heaved a sigh and led Xandie out of the room.

Turning left, she clomped a few steps farther and turned left again before coming to a stop outside a frosted glass door. "This is the side entrance. The front door's closed because most of the staff is at lunch. Take a seat. The receptionist won't be long." She took a few steps and then turned. "The teachers and the office staff are in the break room. If they see you in reception, they'll pop back in." The teenager whistled for a moment. "If someone was digging for dirt on staff and they were quiet, the receptionist wouldn't realize they were there." She winked at Xandie and stomped out of sight, moody dragon hair swinging behind her.

"Sneaky girl." Xandie slipped inside. A glossy wooden bench divided reception from the waiting area. Two desks sat behind the bench with silver filing cabinets next to them. Frosted doors on either side of the desks faced the wooden bench. And both doors were closed. Xandie squinted and made out two body outlines. The receptionists breaking for lunch.

She slid behind the bench and opened a filing cabinet, rifling through the papers, but none of them were staff. She abandoned the first cabinet and moved to the second. This was harder as it was closer to the lunchroom.

Xandie eased the drawer out and skimmed through the files. She'd hit the jackpot, the staff files. She thumbed through until she hit Makepeace.

"You know, Ms. Meyers, I'd have given you any

information if you'd asked. There's no need for surreptitious behavior." A statuesque woman with flowing blonde ringlets towered over Xandie's five-foot-five height.

When in doubt, bluff it out. Xandie frowned and tapped the folder. "I'm disappointed to see the records in such disarray. And have you heard it's the digital age? These could be a fire hazard."

The blonde goddess trilled a laugh. "My goodness, so brazen. I adore you, Alexandra Meyers, and can see why the library picked you." The blonde Amazon slid the file out of Xandie's hand and gave it a fleeting glance before dumping it on a cabinet.

Busted. "Thank you. And you are?" *Please don't work here*, she chanted mentally.

"I'm one of three head mistresses. I'm Melissa Syne, and I'm thrilled to meet you."

Thrilled? Xandie called tall-tale and decided on a blunt attack. "Why are you thrilled? I'm stealing staff files from you."

The woman pointed to the purloined paperwork. "This? There's been a misunderstanding. It's not stealing when it's gifted." She placed the folder into Xandie's sweaty hands.

Xandie sagged against the filing cabinet. All her

thieving adrenaline dissipated in the face of too much sweetness. "Okay, what gives?"

"It devastated us when we lost Sera, but we rejoiced when you accepted your family duties."

"Why is the boss of the academy concerned with what I do?"

"The Great Library was dedicated to the goddesses of the arts. The nine muses. I'm a descendant, as are my two sisters, who run the school with me. Calliope and Clio." She leaned in and whispered conspiratorially, "I'm better equipped to handle teenagers since I'm descended from the muse of tragedy, but don't tell my sisters that." She straightened. "That information needs to be back by the start of the day tomorrow. Do we understand each other, librarian?"

Xandie nodded mutely.

The muse clapped her hands. "Wonderful. Now, we have career day coming up, and we'd love to have you talk about working as the librarian. We'll arrange that later. Goodbye, Alexandra." She propelled Xandie out.

What just happened? Had she met a groupie? Xandie walked determinedly out of the school. She needed to see if her cousins had found any information on Archibald's cause of death. They could go over the school file together. Three heads were better for solving a murder.

———

Lila wiped her sweaty face and heaved in a shuddering breath. "It was horrible. You should have seen her. She fawned over the guy while he cut into Archibald's chest. Holly had to wipe drool off her chin. I puked, and she drooled. I'm shocked at her priorities. Just shocked. Today's youth are so desensitized."

The cousins had gathered in Lila's apartment as Harrow House had too many busybodies and Theo was bathing Horatio, the imp. No one wanted to bear witness to a naked imp.

"I'm two weeks younger than Xandie and four weeks younger than you."

"Exactly. The younger generation." Lila nodded sagely.

Holly responded by pegging a French fry at her cousin's round face.

Lila retaliated with her own food bomb.

Xandie snatched the food before all the delicious oily takeout ended up as missiles. "Besides blood, puke, and drool, did you find anything else?"

"My area of expertise." Holly picked a fry out of her hair and munched. "Someone poisoned Archie. I can't identify it yet since it's only a partial sample."

Xandie groaned. "That's frustrating."

Lila kneeled next to her cousin. "Are you sure she's innocent? Really sure?"

Xandie remembered the remorse on Priss's face after the gnome incident. The sadness and dejection when questioned in her holding cell. "I'm sure. The woman's hiding a secret, but she didn't do it."

"Well, all right then. That's all I need. Let's read her file and see what we can find out?" Lila handed the contents out to everyone.

Dead silence reigned as the three women read through Priss Makepeace's life.

"That was so boring." Lila threw her part on the floor. "Slayer girl has been a fencing instructor for four years. Taught at private colleges in Massachusetts and volunteered at a sporting club for under-privileged sorcerer teenagers. She's a saint."

"Athletic more than saintly," Holly corrected Lila. "She holds national records for fencing as a junior. But once she hit eighteen, she disappeared from competition. Appeared again five years later. I wonder why she disappeared?"

"Her father died." Xandie flapped her sheet of

paper. "The school ran a check. They had trouble getting history on her family, especially her father, Simon, because they moved so often. But when Priscilla Makepeace turned eighteen, her father died. Officials recorded his death as a work-related accident, but it's vague. I think she went to ground, trained, and popped back up as a fencing coach."

"Wow, that's traumatic." Holly teared up.

"But there's something else. Priss told me the academy reached out to her when the permanent instructor went on maternity leave."

"And?" Lila demanded.

"That's a lie. She reached out to them and offered her services. At the exact same time the instructor left on early maternity leave."

Lila pursed her lips. "She paid the other instructor to disappear?"

"Yeah. But why?" Xandie dropped the papers on the chair next to her.

"What about the library?"

"It keeps showing me the same dragon clan migration information. The chapter on the Pennes mentions the heir Adelind and her mate, Ronald. Hang on." Xandie snapped her fingers. "It did mention a missing heir, Melinda Penne, who ran off with a guy of questionable origins."

"What does questionable origins mean?"

"It means he was a dragon slayer." Priss stood in the doorway of Lila's apartment.

Xandie, Lila, and Holly spun around.

"And Melinda Penne was my mother."

SIX

"The twin cops released me on bail this afternoon. I wandered for a while. Then saw the lights on over the bakery. Thought I'd see if you were here." Priss stepped inside.

Xandie peered out the window. Without them realizing, the sun had set while they were going over their evidence.

"Aren't you the only suspect? Why did the cops let you out?" Lila frowned.

She shrugged. "They only took me in for questioning, and they found another print on the poison bottle. They aren't one hundred percent sure I'm the murderer now. They're still investigating. I'm free for now but not off the hook. And I need your help." She shuffled from foot to foot.

Holly threw a cushion. "For God's sake, sit and let the baker feed you."

Priss took a single armchair as Lila jumped up and bustled into the kitchen. She leaned forward. "I'm sorry for not telling the truth, but my life's complicated."

Xandie snorted. "That's an understatement. But at least the library isn't on the fritz. The dragon book it shoved at me mentioned Melinda as a missing heir."

"Not missing, banished. My mom fell in love with a slayer. My father, Simon Makepeace. She tried telling her mother, but Marjorie Penne wouldn't listen. Even her own sisters, Adelind and Belle, turned against her. Adelind's mate Ronald passed on a letter from her mother detailing her banishment." She paused when Lila dumped a large meat and salad sandwich in front of her, along with a glass of milk.

"Eat first. Talk later." She crossed her arms over her chest and waited for Priss to consume her food before she sat.

Priss drained her milk after she finished the sandwich. "Thanks. I appreciate it."

Lila motioned for her to continue her story.

"Ronald broke protocol and gave my parents

money. He apologized, and that was the last time my mom saw her family."

"The library's never wrong. The information mentioned missing, *not* banished. Are you sure you have it right?"

Priss drew a crumpled paper from her pocket. "This is the letter. It's my only proof except for my birth certificate and my parents' marriage certificate. But the rest is at my place. I'm renting at Hazel's bed-and-breakfast on Elm Street."

Xandie grabbed the letter and smoothed it out. It was a handwritten diatribe about Melinda's mate, his dragon-slaying lifestyle, and how the family head refused to countenance such a mate in the family. She'd never allow Melinda and Simon under her roof. Even banished her own daughter and refused to see her again. "Wow, harsh. No way to misunderstand those words. Surely when your mom had you, Marjorie changed her mind?"

"Not that I ever heard. My father said once a dragon's mind was made up, there was little anyone could do to change it. Not even with the tip of a sword."

"Your dad wasn't much of a charmer."

"No." Priss offered a watery smile. "My mother's death ripped a hole inside him. He functioned and took care of me, but he lived and breathed revenge against the dragons. Any dragon. Most of what I learned came from textbooks I hid away from him. As far as the books go, they state dragons are only compatible with other dragons. Human hybrids don't exist."

"Yet clearly, you do." Holly sniffed and dismissed the letter. "Nothing wrong with hybrids. We're extra special; it just takes time for us to find our own way. You have any dragon woo-woo?"

"I can make claws." She held fingers up and concentrated. Sharp silver talons slid out from the tips of her fingers. "And I don't get sick, *ever*. I guess I have dragon immunity, but nothing else so far."

"Rewind. Did your mother even tell Marjorie about you?" Lila arched an eyebrow.

"She was on her way to force her mom to acknowledge me when she collided with a crop duster, outside of town. Both her and the pilot died. That wasn't too long after I was born."

"Point Muse doesn't have crops, so why have a crop duster buzzing overhead?" Lila frowned.

"The investigation into the pilot's death stated he was off course. They suspected he'd been drinking." She stared at her hands. "My dad returned to dragon slaying. He died when I was eighteen. I became a fencing instructor, but I swore I'd get even with my mom's family."

"That's not helping your murder suspect status. Hang on…" Xandie narrowed her gaze. "You're behind the missing artifacts, aren't you? There's a rumor the Pennes had stolen and hoarded them."

"Tried to frame them, but the police never moved against the Pennes. I even snuck into her hoard. But it didn't work. Instead, the cops took me in for questioning." She dropped her head into her hands and moaned. "Everything's such a mess."

"Revenge never wins. Karma always rebounds." Lila intoned the words in a deep voice and then dropped the serious act. "That's what Mom says. On the other hand, Elspeth is a whiz at revenge. That's why the old ducks won't let her enter the annual pie contest any longer."

"Because she kept winning?" What did pie have to do with revenge?

"Nope, because every time the contest came up, Elspeth would bake a pie with a spell mixed in. One year, she had them clucking like ducks, another she laid a truth spell. And don't get Mom started on the chaos caused by the naked spell." She shuddered. "I couldn't eat pie for ages after that."

Xandie ignored Lila's deviation into Elspeth's

whining and asked Priss a question. "Where are the artifacts you stole?" Xandie wondered what other mayhem headed their way.

"I returned the gnome and the lantern. I didn't realize what taking them would cause. There's a snow globe from the gift shop I left in the gallery when Archibald died. Also, a large goblet thing from the funeral home, and I left that in the dragon hoard."

"Oh no." Holly closed her eyes for a moment. "Was it dented and rusted? And larger than a normal cup so that you'd have to use two hands to hold it?"

Priss nodded.

"That's not a goblet. It's a small cauldron."

"How is a small cauldron a problem?" Xandie knew she'd regret asking that question.

"Because the people who run Elysian Fields Funeral Home are necromancers. They collect anything to do with death. The goblet's one of those items." She sagged against the couch, staring off into space.

"For God's sake, Holly. Spit it out. Enough with the dramatics," Lila yelled.

"The goblet is Celtic and belongs to the god Dagda. It can raise the dead."

"Oh, crap." Priss and Xandie mouthed the words together, eyes wide.

"The Cauldron of Dagda had protective spells put on it by Elspeth. I hope stealing it didn't rupture the spells. Or…" She trailed off and then carried on with an audible gulp. "Or Elspeth's killer ceramic gnomes will seem like a garden party compared to supernatural zombie residents."

"Ah, the joy of Point Muse keeps on giving."

"Enough, Lila," Holly snapped at her cousin. Her quiet nature apparently dissolved when confronted by the walking dead.

Xandie stalked to the front window of Lila's apartment and stared out over Main Street. One thing after another. Whoever killed Penne was a step ahead. Frustrated, Xandie laid her forehead against the glass. A red glow behind Main Street caught her attention. "We have another problem."

Lila and Holly ran to Xandie, leaving Priss to follow.

"Near the bed-and-breakfast, wouldn't you say?" Xandie pointed toward the smear of rusty red in the early evening sky.

Lila confirmed Xandie's guess. "Not near. That *is* Hazel's place."

"We need the artifact from the gallery, and we

need to put the fire out at Hazel's. I bet someone set Hazel's alight to destroy any evidence that Melinda had a child." Xandie grabbed Priss and dragged her to the front door. "We'll break into Malones. Harrows, get to Hazel, make sure she's safe, and save our evidence. If we get the globe, we can stop the fire straight away."

Xandie and her new friend headed to the gallery and an icy end to the fire.

"Just one more push. We don't have time to wait." Xandie hung over the windowsill, panting. A sad case of déjà vu shivered along her spine. What was it with windows and her hanging out of them?

Priss slapped a hand on Xandie's behind and gave an almighty shove.

Xandie flew through the window space and collapsed on the floor. Someone had left the window open in a storeroom. Without Priss and her upper body strength, she'd never have clambered inside. "That was too easy."

"Try being on the shoving side. It wasn't so easy."

"I'm ignoring you." Xandie switched her phone's light app on and shone it around the storeroom. "I'll see if I can open a door. Iris really needs a security system."

"No need." Priss eyed the window and backed up. She took a running leap, grabbed hold of the sill, and heaved herself through the open window. Unlike Xandie, the fencing instructor dismounted with grace and then bowed to a pretend audience.

"Hate you and your coordination right now," Xandie grumbled at the way-too-perky murder suspect. "Where's the artifact?"

"In the kitchenette where I found Penne dead. It was in my fencing bag with my workout stuff."

"Why bring your workout gear to an art show?" Xandie slid into the hallway.

"I had a last-minute meeting arranged with Archibald. He caught me at the end of a workout. I had enough time to change but not drop my stuff back at Hazel's. He thought I was lying when I first told him about my mom and being a hybrid. But something must have interested him because he contacted me and asked for a meeting. I went straight to the gallery. And you saw what happened next." She followed Xandie.

"So, why did he want to meet?"

"Some evidence he found made him believe my story. He wanted to help. Stick it to the clan. At least that's what he told me. But then I walked in and stumbled over the poison bottle and earned a stint in jail." She searched the room, looking for her gear. "No bag, no globe. It should be here."

"Unless Iris, the gallery owner, found your bag. Let's search her office."

Priss led the way. "The office is windowless, so we're good for lights." She flicked the switch, and light blazed through the messy, overfilled room. "Iris Malone's a packrat."

Xandie toed a box open. "Mass-produced tourist gifts. Maybe she was selling them as originals?"

"Who knows? I just need my gear." Priss rifled through the other boxes.

Moving boxes aside, Xandie searched through the desk. *Lots of overdue bills, but no bag.* She shoved at a pile of catalogs, and a red leather book hidden in the middle of the stacks slid off the desk. Xandie snatched it before it hit the floor. Her necklace tightened before releasing a second later. The library had been right about the dragon information. Maybe the red journal was important?

"Xandie?"

"I might have found something." She opened the journal and thumbed through the pages. It was a running tally of artifacts. Each entry described the artifact and had a dollar amount, along with two letters. *"Ha."*

"Xandie," Priss called out again.

Spinning, she waved the notebook at Priss. "I found something interesting."

"Ditto." Priss lifted the globe with one hand and a dragon's fang with another.

"Okay, you have a morbid obsession with teeth the same as Holly?"

"I watched Penne drop off boxes to the gallery owner at odd times. I was so focused on getting even, I didn't pay too much attention."

"Sooo?" Xandie drew the word out, waiting for an explanation.

"This fang looks like a dragon tooth. Feels like a dragon to the touch. It might be a side effect of my hybridness, but I know this tooth isn't real. It's not the same one on display the night of the showing. This is a fake."

Bingo. Iris Malone's motive. "This is where the red book comes in." Xandie held up the red journal. "It's a list of artifacts and dollar amounts."

"Malone and Archibald sold dragon artifacts?"

"No, I think they were selling fakes to the suckers in town, then selling the originals on the witch market. There's an initial against each entry.

P.C. I'm sure it stands for Penne clan. They were running a scam right under Ronald Penne's nose. The fight between the two of them was about the scam. Archibald didn't need Iris's contacts anymore. He wanted to sell direct. Iris may have killed him to keep him quiet."

"Wow." Priss looked impressed. "What do we do now?"

Xandie took the journal underarm. "We need to deliver that snow globe to the fire at Hazel's. Then we go to the police and get you off the hook."

Priss pocketed the fake fang before they climbed back through the window.

Daylight dawned on the snowdrift surrounding Hazel's bed-and-breakfast. "Trust you lot to get involved. Zach's gonna lose his shift when he comes back. And you're lucky Ms. Hazel had her naked poker game at the Inn last night." Deputy Melody Braun pouted over her chipped blood-red nail polish before glaring at the Harrows and Priss. "Tell me you didn't set fire to Ms. Hazel's place."

Why do people believe the worst of me? Xandie cleared her throat. "Deputy Braun, we had nothing to do with setting the fire. But we have information that will affect the case of Archibald Penne's death."

Melody Braun groaned. "Another murder? You were almost killed on the last one. Zach was a grizzly the whole time."

Lila smirked. "Chief Braun's a bear shifter, anyway."

"Not a grizzly, we're black bears. Big difference." Melody shifted large, muscled shoulders and glared. "Fine, everyone in. Mother can sort you out."

The girls clambered into the cruiser.

Priss leaned forward and whispered in Xandie's ear, "Her mom's in charge?"

"Trust me. Agatha Braun runs the family and the station with an iron paw." If anyone could sort this out, it was Agatha.

Hopefully, before Police Chief Zach Braun stuck his oh-so-appealing nose in.

SEVEN

"Let me get this straight." Agatha Braun ran a calloused hand through her frizzy gray, chin-length bob. "Makepeace here is innocent of murder. You broke into the gallery, found evidence of Iris Malone and Archibald Penne running an art fraud black-market business. And you think Iris killed Penne and firebombed Hazel's because there was evidence there of Makepeace as a long-lost Penne heir?"

Priss laid out her letter in front of Agatha. "This was written by Marjorie and banishes my mom. She never wanted to see her again."

"Bull poop. Marjorie Penne adored Melinda. She wouldn't care if your father was a serial killer. She'd never have banished her."

"My dad was a dragon slayer. Apparently, that

tipped her over into banishing my mother." Priss laid a hand on the desk. "Mom tried to come back after she had me to tell Marjorie but never made it. She collided with a crop duster outside of town."

Agatha sat back in a chair and crunched on a beef jerky strip. "That was during old man Wolf's reign of terror. My mate, the previous police chief, was away on a joint task force. Wolf was acting chief. He made such a mess of things in Point Muse the paranormal investigator group was called in for clean-up duty. But I'm telling you—no way would Marjorie cut Melinda off."

Xandie leaned forward, putting as much unwavering trust for Priss as she could dredge up into her voice. "Agatha, Priss didn't kill Archibald. Trust us. Malone is in it up to her money-hungry armpits. We just need time to find the evidence to prove it. That's all we ask."

Agatha slapped her desk. "All you had to do was ask, sweet Xandie. Why, I think of you as a daughter-in-law." Agatha winked as Xandie flushed bright red.

Priss dumped all the evidence in front of Agatha. "Thank you, Mrs. Braun."

Agatha smiled at Priss. "You know, you do look a little like your momma. In fact, I think you have Marjorie's stubborn chin. Now scatter, the lot of you.

And stay away from Malone; we'll track her down. Now get." She flapped a hand at the two women to encourage them to leave.

As the girls trundled out of the station, a worried Priss whispered to Xandie, "*Can* she help me?"

"There's not much that gets past Agatha Braun. She just needs evidence to make it stick."

All they had to do was track down Iris Malone...

***

"Two days, Theo. Two days of patiently waiting." Xandie shelved a book with extra oomph. "All Agatha tells me is to shut it. She'll call me when she has something concrete on Malone's location. The wait is driving me crazy." Xandie blew her hair away from her face.

"So what? Not your place to hunt Malone down. Take her advice." Theo ran his tongue over Horatio's hairless head. The imp chattered to Theo as the cat groomed him.

"Priss and Lila are doing okay rooming together. But who knows how long Lila's good mood will last?" Xandie moved a pile of books off the desk and opened the appointment book. "Right, library, let's go." Xandie flicked to the requests for admittance and wrote them into the book. The library decided whom it wanted inside it. Some of the requests disappeared and then appeared written at different times during the week. Some were noted information only. Those requests meant Xandie had to dig the information out and copy it. The library then sent it on.

Xandie ducked as a scroll flew overhead to land with a skid on the library desk. Grabbing it, Xandie headed to the office to copy the scroll. "Mating practices of a Basilisk is done and dusted." Xandie shuddered at the thought of mating with a lizard that killed with a look.

The library phone rang, shocking Xandie from the images of a basilisk mating. Her hand flew to her chest as her heartbeat raced. The ley lines around the town interfered with phones and Internet reception. She'd become used to the silence as opposed to the constant strident ringtones of her phone. Elspeth had a charm to ensure phone reception, but her grandmother wasn't a fan of sharing. Snickering at her silliness, Xandie grabbed the phone. "Xandie Meyers. How can I help you?"

"I need to talk to the old broad. Put her on the phone, would you?"

Low, gravelly, smoke-a-pack-a-day male tones

flowed through the line. By old broad did he mean her late great-aunt? "Do you mean Sera Meyers?"

"What I said. Time is money, girl. Hurry it up."

Xandie narrowed her gaze and drummed her nails on the library desk. No one over twenty and under sixty enjoyed being called girl, and at twenty-five, she was no exception. What made it worse is that now she had to explain to a complete stranger about Sera's death. "I'm sorry, but Sera died a few months ago. I'm her great-niece, Xandie."

"Scandinavian skipping skunks." The man cursed a blue steak. "The old girl owed me. I've spent time and money on this case."

Case? What on earth was the weird swearing man rambling about? "I have no clue what case you're talking about. Sera never mentioned anything before she was killed."

Dead silence filled the line for a moment.

"Killed? Huh, I'm not surprised. That librarian had a cranky streak and held a grudge more than any troll woman I've ever dated. But she was a good poker player. Respect for that."

"You knew she was a librarian?"

"I'm a troll, not a moron. It's my job to know my clients. I'm a private investigator at Trollish Investigations Inc. *You lose 'em, we find 'em.*"

What the heck would Sera need an investigator for when she had the library?

"Say, you said your name was Meyers, right?"

Xandie's skin prickled, and she adjusted the phone in her hand, wary at the troll's sudden interest. "Yes, why?"

"That's the case. The old girl had me looking into your mother, Miranda Harrow's disappearance."

Stiffening, Xandie's breath caught momentarily. "My mother's disappearance was twenty years ago. When did Sera contact you?"

"Six months ago. She wanted the investigation kept quiet. She paid half my fee up front and the rest was payable on delivery of my findings."

Xandie's thoughts raced as she tried to make sense out of his words. Why would Sera get a private investigator years after her mother's disappearance? Why six months ago? "Why would Sera contact you now?"

The troll sighed on the other end of the phone. "Look, love. All I know is what the librarian told me about the case. Something had come up recently that had her thinking about the chick. She wanted me to look into it. So, what about the rest of my money?"

Had Sera realized the Knights of Sanguis had caused Miranda Harrow's death, or was it something else? "If Sera owed you money, the library will pay it. But it's pointless now. We know the Knights of Sanguis caused her death."

"Her supposed death, you mean. I heard about the Knight murders in Point Muse. Nice catch of the killer, by the way. Maybe you should be a P.I."

Supposed death? Xandie blinked back tears. She'd finally come to terms with the loss of her mother. Now this pushy troll was throwing words like "supposed" into the mayhem of her world. "The knight chased my mother off a cliff. I think that's pretty definitive, don't you? Plus, what mother would desert her child for that long?"

"In my line of work, you'd be surprised. All kinds of lowlifes out there. In fact, with your case…"

Xandie cut off the troll's words with a growl through gritted teeth. "My mother was not a lowlife."

"Hey, no offense." The troll backpedaled. "I was gonna say your mother's case was different. But you cut me off. I'm just saying there's some questions raised about the circumstances around your mother's disappearance. It's all in my file if you want it?"

Do I? She'd buried her mother, figuratively and literally. Especially if you counted the memorial service her father had held in Andrews, seven years after her mother was declared legally dead. The

Harrows had probably had something in Point Muse too. But if there were questions unanswered, maybe she should look at the file. "Fine, send it. Send an invoice. You'll get your money when the library deposits it."

"That's the way to do business, sweetheart. I'll be in touch when the gold clears my account at Witch and Creature Financial Holdings." The troll hung up without another word.

Lowering the phone, Xandie stared at it as if it were a snake ready to strike. The pit of her stomach churned, a mess of knotted feelings. She thought she'd solved her mother's death, but now Sera and that damn troll had cracked open a can of emotional worms again. Xandie dropped the phone and laid her head against a wall. "I still have Archibald's murder to solve and Priss's name to clear. I don't need this."

"What was all that about?" Theo glared at Xandie, the grooming of his pet imp forgotten in the hunt for gossip.

Xandie cleared her throat and faced her feline guardian, unsure just how much to tell him. Like everyone else, he thought the case of her missing mother was finally solved. Now with the troll P.I's investigation, the events surrounding her mother looked murky again. Plus, he always worried she'd do something stupid and leave the library without its librarian. "Some troll looking for Sera. He didn't realize she'd died." Xandie busied herself tidying scrolls, unable to meet Theo's gaze.

"And the rest?"

"Nothing, like I said. He wanted to speak to Sera about private business."

"You're a bad liar, librarian. Now spill," Theo hissed and slammed a paw down, narrowly missing Horatio.

"Fine." Xandie threw her hands in the air and stomped to the couch next to Theo. "He *was* a troll and *was* looking for Sera. But he's also a private investigator. Sera had him looking into my mom's disappearance."

"Was it so hard to tell me the whole truth?" Theo sniffed his disdain at her antics.

"Did you know Sera was investigating my mother?"

"I knew she'd always had doubts about Miranda Harrow's disappearance. Six months ago, she changed her routine. Would disappear for a few hours at a time. She'd get super-secret phone calls at all hours. I thought she was going senile." Theo stretched and then jumped off the chair to pace the floor.

"What kind of doubts? At the time, the police thought Mom had run off. What were Sera's suspicions?"

"Sera and the Harrows swore Miranda would never leave you. They thought she'd had an accident."

"Well, I guess in a way she did. The knight chased her until she fell off a cliff." Xandie grimaced, then stared off into space.

"So, what's the problem with this troll guy? You already know what happened to her."

"Do we? I explained about the knight, but he said there were still unanswered questions surrounding her supposed death. 'Supposed,' Theo, that's the word he used. What if there's another reason for her disappearance?"

"Sounds like you're grasping at straws. You're a librarian, so act like it. Do your research. This guy could be a scam artist."

"Thanks for your feline advice, but if there's a chance he has more information on my mom, I have to take it. Still, you have a good point about research." Xandie leapt up and rapped on the wooden desk. "Library, do you have any information on the company Trollish Investigations Inc.?"

A thick green book rattled on a bookshelf near the window overlooking the garden.

Rushing over, Xandie snatched the book up and rifled through it before exclaiming in victory as she flashed the page at Theo. "See, he's listed in the top five hundred reputable otherworldly private investigators in North America."

Theo snorted. "Doesn't mean he's legit. Just means he can tick and flick boxes to appear above board."

Xandie slammed the book shut. "I've made up my mind. He'll contact me once the library deposits the rest of his fee. I'm meeting with him."

The library's lights dimmed to a muted glow.

"See?" Xandie pointed to the roof. "She agrees with me. So, suck it up, kitty cat."

The power flickered off and on with a crack and a sizzle, punctuating Xandie's words.

She rubbed a hand over the surface of the library wall. "Have a nap, library. Theo will let you know if there's an issue." Ever since the library had rushed to her rescue the last time she'd tried to solve a murder, the poor supernatural entity had labored. The massive amount of energy it used to change itself to save Xandie had depleted its inner power core. For now, the library had to nap like an old woman to fill up its energy well.

Xandie shooed Theo and Horatio out the door. "Get some rest, library. We need to focus on solving the dragon murder before delving into the troll's case file. You need to keep your energy up." She shut the door behind her and sagged against the wood. "Meanwhile, I'm still stuck waiting for Agatha to track down Iris Malone. Argh. One step forward, two steps back." Just like her life in general in Point Muse.

A pounding on her front door shocked Xandie, and she jumped and squealed. Grumbling at herself, she stalked down the hallway and flung the front door open. And was greeted by the sight of a morose dragon teenager faking a nonthreatening smile. "Do you need something, Es?" The dragon teen rocked back and forth, hands clasped behind her back. Her long silver and black hair flew out behind her.

"Hi, Ms. Meyers."

Es was plainly on her best behavior, if the fake smile was anything to go by. But Xandie noted silver and green iridescent scales flickered to life in random patterns on her skin. Maybe Es wasn't as calm as she was projecting. A flash of silver scales surfaced along her jawline. Xandie tried to put her at ease. "You can call me Xandie. Can I help with anything?"

Es sighed and produced a gold and silver business card. "My father asked if you would meet him and my mother at Mayweather Inn for a drink at midday today. They want to speak to you." Her fake smile fell away, and her normally surly attitude appeared. "I only agreed to ask because they wouldn't get off my back. So, my job is done. I could care less if you turn up or not." Es spun to leave but paused for a moment. "My parents don't do anything without a reason. Especially my father. Be careful what you agree to." Es strode off and flicked the card behind her.

Xandie bent down and picked up the glossy card. Adeline and Ronald Penne was engraved in gold-embossed type across the front of the silver gloss card. Ostentatious was the theme. She wondered what the dragon socialites were after. And why did Es Penne warn Xandie about her own parents? Xandie checked her watch. "Only one way to find out."

A drink with the social elite of Point Muse, it was.

EIGHT

"Why, Alexandra, dear. What a lovely surprise."

Rose Mayweather's grimace said anything but. The woman had hated Xandie's great-aunt Sera because a demon professor had preferred Sera to her. Aphrodite's descendant wasn't the forgive and forget type when it came to matters of the heart.

"Hi, Rose." Xandie offered a small smile. She had no clue where the Pennes were, either the bar or the dining room. But she'd bet members of the high society of Point Muse wouldn't be caught dead in the bar.

"Are you on your own or meeting your cousins?"

Silent code for you can't be meeting a man. "I'm supposed to meet Adelind and Ronald Penne for a drink."

Rose coughed into her hand. "Oh, sweetie, Adelind would never meet you for a drink here."

Xandie produced the Pennes' glossy business card. "Es Penne invited me this morning."

"Like I said, you won't be meeting the Penne heir. But good old Ronald is in the bar." Rose gestured to the frosted door on the left. "He's sitting in the back, in one of the booths." She turned away but spun back. "Word to the wise, Alexandra. Ronald's smooth and slick, and people always find themselves doing what he wants in the end. Be careful what you agree to." With a swish of her nineteen fifties style petticoats, Rose sashayed into the dining room opposite.

"That's encouraging," Xandie murmured to herself. She pushed the door to the bar open and blinked furiously, adjusting to the dimly lit interior.

The bar was more elegant than she'd expected from a descendant of Aphrodite. Comfortable, plush leather chairs dotted the space, and plain dark wood and black steel tables filled the room. Muted lighting encouraged an intimate atmosphere without over-powering. Brass pendants hung from the ceiling and gave the room a metallic, cool ambience. Nothing tacky about the bar at Mayweather Inn.

Xandie headed for the bar and asked for a soda. When facing a smooth operator, impaired senses weren't the way to go. Reaching for her drink with a nod of thanks to the bartender, Xandie turned and faced the seating area. Scanning for a lone dragon, Xandie nearly threw her drink in the air when someone tapped her shoulder.

"Apologies, Ms. Meyers. I didn't mean to scare you." A polished older man offered a self-deprecating smile.

"Mr. Penne, I take it?" Xandie brushed droplets of liquid off her plain blue shirt. The high society dragon would have to take her as she was. Jeans and a clean shirt were the best clothing she owned nowadays. Business wear had gone out the window after she quit working at her father's college library.

"Yes, I am. Would you care to take a seat in the back?" Not waiting for an answer, he nodded to the bartender and strode toward a table in an extra shadowed corner of the room.

"Of course, Mr. Penne, no problem." Xandie arched an eyebrow and followed. So far, Mr. Penne wasn't that impressive.

He waited for Xandie to settle into a chair and gestured to the bartender for his drink, taking a long sip once delivered. An obviously expensive glass of red wine for a man with expensive taste.

Xandie refused to breach their silent consideration of each other. He wanted her here, so he could talk first.

Giving in, Ronald Penne opened the conversation. "You're wondering why I called for a meeting?"

"I was wondering why you had your daughter deliver the invitation and when your wife will be joining us."

"Ah, yes, Esmeralda." The dragon moved his wine glass around the table, transfixed by the glow of red liquid through the glass. "She's at a difficult age and frankly the only person she listens to is my mother-in-law, Marjorie. But for some reason, you interest her. I allowed her to deliver the message for that reason." He stared straight at Xandie and smiled, a practiced twist of the lips with an expected outcome.

One she wasn't interested in. "And your wife, Adelind?"

Ronald coughed slightly. "Adelind doesn't care for the ambience of Mayweather Inn. She's happy to let me deal with business."

Now we're getting somewhere. Xandie politely refused another drink from the bartender and leaned forward. "And what kind of business are we doing today, Mr. Penne?"

Ronald glanced around the room and lowered his voice. "It's about the gallery and Archibald."

"You mean the art fraud and black-market scam Archibald Penne and Iris Malone had going on with dragon artifacts?"

Ronald Penne looked surprised at how much Xandie knew. Recovering, he continued, "Yes. I had no clue when Marjorie ordered me to help with the gallery what was happening."

"Marjorie ordered you to oversee the gallery project?" Why would Marjorie want all their dragon artifacts on show? Not to mention selling them. Marjorie Penne was cranky, closemouthed, and preferred to stay out of the limelight. According to Es, Adelind and Ronald dealt with anything that was social-related. So, why bring the spotlight to the Penne clan by selling off family artifacts?

"I don't understand why she did it. It's not as if the clan needs money." Ronald downed his red wine in a long swallow. He flicked his finger for another. "My mother-in-law always has a reason for every-thing she does. But the last few months, she's become erratic. Forgetting things and becoming secretive."

Dragon dementia? Wouldn't Es have mentioned

it if Marjorie were losing her dragon marbles? "Are you saying she knew about Archibald selling fake artifacts? Selling the originals on the black-market?"

He nodded glumly. "I think so. I heard them arguing. Not long before Archibald died. He wanted more money. I had no clue what he was raving about, and then he turned up dead."

Everyone seemed to have an issue with Archibald, not to mention a motive. Not a popular guy. "You think Marjorie had something to do with the artifacts and Archibald's death?"

"All I know is artifacts have disappeared from the Penne hoard. Yet others that have nothing to do with the clan have appeared." He paused for a sip of his newly delivered red wine. "Some of the artifacts that have disappeared from around town might be in our hoard. I know I saw a pipe that isn't ours. In fact, I think it might even be a Harrow family artifact." He looked expectantly at Xandie.

She shrugged. "I have no clue what Elspeth or the others might have squirreled away, but I can ask. Have you told anyone else about this?"

"Adelind, as she's the heir, but she doesn't want to move without evidence." Ronald looked ashamed for a moment. "I've left anonymous tips for the police, but they're as scared as Adelind is to move against Marjorie."

"Iris Malone and Archibald argued before he died. He told her he wanted out. I get the feeling he wanted to branch out on his own. Cut out the middle person. What do you think?"

"I wouldn't have been surprised. He was ambitious. And Marjorie has a short fuse."

Xandie tapped her fingers on the table. "We now have Marjorie and Iris as suspects."

"What about the suspect the police arrested? Priscilla Makepeace? She was found over Archibald's body. Or so I heard." Ronald narrowed his gaze on Xandie. "Or do you have other information?"

Ignoring his question, Xandie posed her own. "Have you heard of any Penne hybrids?"

Ronald paused for a moment and chuckled. "It's common knowledge, dragons are incompatible with other species. There's no way there are any Penne hybrids polluting the gene pool."

Xandie wrinkled her nose. Prejudiced much? *If you ain't dragon, you ain't.* "What if Melinda Penne had a child? If her mate had some kind of latent dragon DNA? Could it be possible?"

Ronald Penne drew himself up. Every line of his body bristled with offense. "Dragon hybrids are not possible, especially from a dragon slayer. Marjorie banished Melinda because she refused to give him up. I'm sorry about her death. But there is no way Priscilla Makepeace is her daughter." Angry, Ronald stood and drained his wine. "I asked you here to help me get to the bottom of Archibald's murder. You have a reputation for that type of thing." He sneered the last few words out before continuing, "Obviously, it's beyond your human capabilities—"

A woman broke into his tirade, silencing him mid word. "Ronald. I've tried to contact you numerous times. But you haven't answered." A tall, emaciated, silver-haired woman glared at him.

Looking flustered, Ronald pasted a smile on his face. "Adelind. I apologize; I was having a meeting with the librarian, Alexandra Meyers. This is my wife, Adelind."

Xandie smiled sweetly. This was Es Penne's mother and the current heir to the Penne clan. "Nice to meet you, Adelind."

Adelind Penne ran her gaze over Xandie's disheveled brown hair and snagged on her holey blue jeans. Baring her teeth in a perfunctory grimace of greeting, Adelind nodded to Xandie.

"Librarian. Esmeralda's quite complimentary about you."

"Hard to imagine Es being complimentary about anyone," Xandie replied with a wry smile. For a moment, Adelind's face softened at the mention of the pouty dragon teenager before sliding back into bland dragon face.

"Es can be difficult at times." Dismissing Xandie, Adelind focused on Ronald. "Belle has been notified. She'll be flying in for Archibald's funeral. Please make sure the arrangements are made at the compound for her and whatever playboy she brings with her."

Belle Penne. Archibald's mother. "Will the town be able to attend the funeral? He was well-liked." *Surely, the killer would be at the funeral. Gloating over his misdeeds.*

"There will be a ceremony at the funeral home followed by a private family one. Details will be forthcoming and—" Adelind squealed mid-sentence and leapt onto a chair.

The old girl was surprisingly agile. Xandie peered under the table, wondering what had set the dragon off. The high-pitched trill of a pipe had Xandie wincing and covering her ears. A line of gray fur wound its way through the bar. Patrons screamed or jumped on chairs. Xandie lowered her hands and straightened as a river of rats charged at her. Skittering nails on wood floors beat any horror movie special effects for maximum impact. A rat launched itself at Xandie as the pack marched past.

"Argh," Xandie screeched and joined the panicked dragon. Standing on a chair next to her.

Ronald had already shifted away from the mass of writhing rodents and used the booth as a barrier. He shoved a chair in the way of the rats. "What do we do, librarian?" he screamed at Xandie.

"I am not a pest exterminator. Use your dragon kung fu and take them out," Xandie hollered back. A grayish-white rat with evil red eyes ran up the couch toward her. Without thinking, Xandie shot out a foot and punted it away. Right into the silvery, shoulder-length hair of an already hysterical dragon.

The same Adelind Penne who, without a thought, belched radioactive dragon breath at the rats. Xandie gagged as the bitter smell of singed fur and skin hit the back of her throat. The rest of the rats whirled around and scooted out of the bar. Except the one that still struggled, entangled, in Adelind's hair.

"I am so sorry." Xandie stepped over to the

dragon and tried to untangle the rodent, but the Penne heir bared her teeth.

"Ronald." Adelind hissed her husband's name.

Ronald Penne appeared from the side of the booth and helped his wife down from the couch. He extended a wicked sharp claw and speared the rat. He drew it from its dragon hair nest and flung it on the floor where he stomped on the animal, cracking its back with an audible snap.

Adelind stormed out without a sideways glance at her husband or Xandie.

"I told you I saw a pipe in the Penne hoard. Now do you believe me?" He swept a hand over the mess of dead rats left behind.

"How can a pipe make rats attack us?"

Now she knew why Es avoided her parents. *Xandie* wanted to avoid Adelind and Ronald pronto.

"Are you dense? The pipe belonged to the Pied Piper of Hamlin." He paused, waiting for a reaction. "He called the rats and led them out of town? It's a Brothers Grimm tale. And it belongs to Elspeth Harrow. You need to do something about this before the clan decides you are no longer suitable for your position." With that threat, he left, picking his way through the dead rat minefield.

Xandie grabbed hold of the side of the booth and

slid to a seat. She had no choice. Her position as the librarian was, once again, under fire.

"Bartender, I'll take that drink now." Xandie slumped and stared off into space.

Some days, she wished she could go back to being a plain old human...

Some days.

NINE

"Dragon stalking is a thing with the youngsters now, hey?" Elspeth hip-shoved her daughter, Amelia, out of the way and settled in front of the window.

Amelia scowled and stomped over next to her sister, Winifred.

"Surveillance, not stalking." Holly adjusted the blinds of the bakery picture window, then opened the gap to peer out at Main Street.

"Surveillance, court order. Same thing." Elspeth waved the definition away and guzzled from a rhinestone-bedazzled flask.

"And that's why you're not allowed within a hundred meters of old man Herb."

"Lila Harrow, you know full well I was just brushing a bee off him."

Lila threw her hands up in disgust. "He was inside the church at the time, and it was a fly, not a bee."

"It could have been a bee. I'm old. I get confused." Elspeth cackled and snapped her fingers like a crab's pincers. "Besides, you'd think a descendant of Hercules would have some gumption."

Amelia, Elspeth's oldest daughter, covered her eyes and breathed long and slow before opening and focusing on her daughter, Lila. "She won't listen. Just give in and practice your apologies to the town. That's what we do."

Priss snorted her coffee, spraying the back of Xandie's neck. "Wish she was my grandmother," Priss whispered to Xandie.

Wiping the back of her neck, Xandie took a sip of hot chocolate. She was used to people's reactions when they met Elspeth. Wouldn't be the first time someone sprayed drink on her over Elspeth's antics. Her mother had never mentioned the Harrows, Elspeth, or anyone from Point Muse. It was as if the woman had blotted out her past and made herself over to make her husband happy. *And that was the problem.*

Xandie was five when her mother disappeared,

but she still had memories of their family. Of her mother and father cuddling in the kitchen or having a picnic outside. It was only after Miranda Harrow's disappearance that her father had become the emotionless, pompous librarian she knew now. Xandie stared at the table, tracing the cracks in the surface over and over.

"Try living with her." Holly grimaced and added, "Or my mother. The dead are more restful than those two together."

"You're spending time with the wrong dead people, sweetie. Trust me, some of them are real partiers."

"A penny for them, cousin?" Lila tapped the table to get Xandie's attention.

"Not sure about the value of my thoughts yet. I'll let you know."

"Are you okay, Xandie?"

She grimaced. "I'm okay." Xandie made a decision and leaned close to Lila, lowering her voice. "I took a call from a troll investigator a couple days ago. Sera paid him to investigate my mother's death."

Lila whistled. "Wow, I had no clue Sera had done that. What did he say?"

"That's the thing. He wanted the rest of his fee

and told me he had a file on my mom. I did tell him about the Sanguis knight, but he said there were still unanswered questions about her death. Well, he called it *supposed* death."

"What will you do?"

"Pay him his money, I guess."

"And the file?"

"What file are you nattering about, favorite grandchild?" Elspeth raised her voice from where she stood at the window.

Lila shook her head and yelled back, "A file about your criminal activities. Xandie's connected. She knows all about your scams."

"The dead tell no tales." Elspeth smirked and turned dramatically, pointing a painted nail, complete with a skull etched on it, at Xandie. "Are we spying or not? I got things a'brewing."

Xandie flashed a small smile of thanks at Lila for her misdirection. Then she settled her drink on the table and joined her family at the bakery window. "Dragons have been coming in the last two days since the rat incident." Xandie shot an accusing glare at Elspeth, putting her mother's death and the troll's investigation on the back burner. *For now.*

"Hex me. I forgot I had the pipe. It's not my fault." Elspeth dramatically threw her hands up.

"It's not your fault you collect cursed objects used to attack your granddaughter?" Lila wondered out loud.

"Depends on the granddaughter, I guess." Elspeth bared her teeth, chuckling to herself.

"Sometimes, Mother, I wonder why we haven't been run out of town with flaming torches." Winifred sniffed a cotton wedge of material soaked in lavender oil.

"They wouldn't dare. I know where all the bodies are buried, of course." Elspeth took a drag from her hip flask again before turning to Priss. "So, halfling, you met the dragon bi..." Elspeth coughed. "Ah, dragon beast? The head honcho, Marjorie, yet?"

"No. I'm kind of avoiding dragons right now. The police have cleared me officially of being a suspect in Archibald's death, though."

"Considering the dragon jam out the front, I think you'll be able to blend in with the crowd at the funeral anyway." Elspeth nodded at the backup of black cars jamming Main Street, waiting for the one stoplight in town to change.

Xandie checked her watch. "We have an hour before the funeral starts. Plenty of time to head back to Harrow house and change into our funeral finery."

Elspeth pushed away from the window and

exclaimed grandly, "I decided my grandchildren would benefit from my protection at the funeral. I even have my special cape washed and ready to go." She lowered her raised arms and paused, as if waiting for the gratitude to pour forth.

Holly groaned and begged her mother, Winifred, with pleading hands outstretched, "Mom, please. Not the *cape*."

"Now, now, dear. If your grandmother wants to be involved in your lives, we have to encourage it." Winifred smile beatifically at her daughter. "Especially when it's your lives, not ours."

Amelia smiled and agreed. "She's your responsibility now. Just don't take your eyes off her and that hip flask. She doesn't know when to say no."

Everyone turned and stared at Elspeth, surprising her mid chug. "What can I say? You're here for a good time, not a long time." She jiggled her flask, listening for a lack of slosh. "Anyone got any witchshine I can top this up with?"

Xandie couldn't help thinking Archibald's funeral wasn't going to end well.

"Pink velvet hooded cape with pockets isn't exactly funeral attire or blendy." Xandie created a new word on the spot as she stared gob-smacked at her grandmother's attire.

"Elspeth doesn't do subtle." Lila rolled her eyes at her grandmother's antics. "You should have realized that when you saw her name bedazzled on the back of the cape."

Xandie muttered under her breath, "Someone needs to kill that bedazzler permanently."

"Can't." Holly shook her head. "She enchanted it. Any time someone other than Elspeth touches it, the damn thing screams blue murder. We've given up on the sabotage attempts."

Elspeth sidled up to a crony and offered her the flask. The fluorescent pink-haired octogenarian glanced around and then chugged a healthy portion of the liquid before passing it back. The women cackled together and slunk off to hunt down more cronies for their coven of bright-haired flask drinkers.

Priss shook her head in amazement. "I can honestly see Elspeth taking over a small country and establishing her own dictatorship based on the religion of hip flask drinking."

"I think she did that when she was young already." Lila hooked arms with Priss and casually ambled around the crowded side lawn of the Elysian Fields Funeral Home.

Grecian columns, white stone, and marble covered the funeral home. "It looks like a Greek temple," Xandie whispered to Holly as they moved around other funeral goers.

"It was founded by a Greek guy called Charon. Now his descendants run the place. Hector and Hillary are brother and sister and both necromancers. I've learned a lot from them." Holly smiled slightly and patted a column. "The place grows on you."

Xandie hid the shiver that ran along her spine. A funeral home wasn't a place she'd ever get used to. But with Holly being part banshee, death was a normal event for her. "Have we spotted Marjorie yet?"

Priss dropped back to Xandie and Holly and pointed at the altar of wood built to house the body of Archibald atop it. "Archibald's mom arrived earlier. She's standing with Marjorie near where Archibald is laid out."

A curvy, silver-haired blonde fashion plate in a dark magenta pantsuit stood near the Penne family matriarch, shaking hands with a funeral guest.

"Apparently, the dragons burn their fallen on a

wooden platform. The head of the family uses her flames to set it on fire. Sort of like a Viking burial, I guess." Priss shrugged, pretending her non-interest.

"Marjorie looks like an iron maiden." Lila walked up and snuggled between Holly and Xandie. "Dark gray pantsuit. Check. Every strand of her silver bob in place. Check. Make up. Check. Requisite scowl. *Check. Check. Check.*"

Xandie fought the urge to stand up for the grieving grandmother. "She just lost her grandson. Murdered. I can't imagine she'd be happy to socialize."

"My grandmother hates socializing at any time, but she loves a good game of poker. Elspeth's a regular visitor to the compound." Es Penne popped up, without warning, next to Xandie.

"Figures. Elspeth loves fleecing rich people." Holly snorted.

Xandie smiled at the idea of Elspeth fleecing a dragon.

"Not much fleecing going on. I think they just love gossiping about everyone," Es whispered to Xandie. "I couldn't find that cup or cauldron thing you told me about. But there are plenty of things in Gran's hoard that don't belong to us. What do we do?" Es looked worried for her gran as she fiddled with the flounces of the high-neck black Victorian blouse she'd paired with tight black pants and chunky combat boots.

"Just keep an eye out for Marjorie. The police still haven't found Iris yet. Maybe everything will be fine," Xandie offered hopefully.

"There's a locked door in the hoard room. I couldn't get into it. I'll pick the lock after the funeral and have a look." Es raised a hand to her grandmother and drifted off in her family's direction.

"She seems to be coping okay." Priss nodded in the direction of the teenager.

Lila agreed. "I don't think they were close. Archibald was a lot like his mother, Belle. Always looking for the next big payout. There wasn't much love lost between him and Es. She's a teenager, and he couldn't see any way to use her yet. At least that's the impression she gave me."

Xandie watched the way Es hovered over her grandmother and ignored her aunt. "No love lost there either. I'd have thought Adelind and Ronald would be here socializing up a storm."

Holly casually pointed to the left of the funeral home. Adelind and Ronald, not a hair out of place after the rat attack, were having a heated exchange.

"Love to be a fly on the wall for that conversation." Xandie would have traded Theo to hear what the couple argued about. Adelind finished talking and flicked her husband's hand off her arm before storming elegantly off to stand with her family. Ronald adjusted his dove gray tie and disappeared out to the car park.

"Now where is he heading off to?" Xandie's musings were cut short as Marjorie Penne stepped forward and held up a hand for quiet.

"Thank you to everyone, both Point Muse residents and others, for attending today to celebrate Archibald Henry Penne's life and death." Marjorie paused for a moment, her stone facade crumbling at the edges. She pulled herself together and continued, "Our clan has specific cultural requirements for a funeral that will be carried out in private later. Please join us in honoring our clan member with respect and compassion. Of course, refreshments will also be offered at Penne house afterward." Marjorie stopped speaking as Adelind whispered into her ear. She cleared her throat and continued, "Limited refreshments. Thank you." The Penne clan stepped back toward the wooden bier holding Archibald's body.

The throng of mourners surged forward, gathering around Archibald. Xandie and the girls were swept up with everybody else.

"Holly, what does the Cauldron of Dagda look like?" Lila frowned, peering out at Archibald.

"I told you. Round, rusty, raises the dead." Holly rolled her eyes.

"You mean the same rusty round thing that's currently clutched in Archibald's dead, unmoving hands?"

"What?" Holly squeaked the word and shook her head, mumbling, "No. No. Not happening. Dead is dead." Holly rocked back and forth on her feet, hands over her eyes.

Xandie pulled Holly's hands away from her face. "Not the time to close your eyes, Holly. When the crowd realizes what's happening, there will be a stampede."

Sightless, silver eyes met Xandie's stare. Holly's banshee genes had activated in the middle of a funeral. "The dead will drink from the un-dry cauldron. Sipping on life while devouring the flesh." Holly intoned the words before shrieking loudly.

Mourners around them moved away from Holly when they heard the shriek. Banshees had appeared in Point Muse before, just never in the middle of a funeral for a murdered dragon.

Lila rubbed her cousin's back. "Holly, you okay?"

Holly grimaced. "Yeah, that hasn't happened before. Normally, I see people dying. I do not have full-on speaking visions."

"Who's a good death girl?" Elspeth hung an arm around Holly's neck and squeezed her in a one-armed hug. "I knew the Harrow blood would come through that wimpy banshee stuff. Proud of you. Have a drink."

Elspeth shoved the hip flask at Holly.

Surprised, Holly took a sip and stared, shocked, at Elspeth. "That isn't witchshine. That's iced tea."

Elspeth snatched the flask back. "Quiet, you'll ruin the cred. Besides, do you really think I'd drink while on protection duty?"

"What cred, Elspeth? The crazy, chaotic, moonshine-guzzling hex-making grandmother Harrow we all know and love? *Kind of.*" Lila grabbed the flask, took her own swig.

"Yeah, that cred," Elspeth growled and took the flask back, hiding it in her sagging cleavage. She twitched the pink velvet cloak back over her head. "Now, where's the waking dead guy?"

Xandie gestured to the front where the crowd had now backed away from Archibald's twitching body. "We think he has the Cauldron of Dagda.

Holly told us it had disappeared from the necromancers who owned it."

Elspeth hitched up her pants and dragged out something that had been hidden underneath her cloak. She threw bottles filled with salt at her granddaughters. "Arms up, girlies. We're going into battle." Elspeth cracked her knuckles.

Holly grinned. "Of course, salt. Salt purifies the living and the dead, and it breaks the connection to the cauldron. You're amazing, Gran." Holly hugged Elspeth tight.

"Harrow blood will out, sweet pea. That's the Harrow vision you had." Elspeth patted Holly on the back and extricated herself from the hug. "Now let's kill dead people."

"Elspeth? There's only Archibald. We don't need all these bottles of salt for just him." Xandie held out her bottle.

Cackling, Elspeth pointed over Xandie's shoulder at the group of dead people currently shambling toward the funeral bier. Mourners finally noticed, and screams rang out around the grassy area. People scattered in every direction. Elspeth took off toward the group of walking dead, yelling over a shoulder, "Get the cauldron off Archibald and salt it." Elspeth backed up and then sped off at a pace belying her age.

Xandie watched her octogenarian grandmother take a ninja leap into a gaggle of the walking dead.

"*Geronimo.*"

TEN

Xandie ducked between mourners as she raced for a dead man who stopped to terrorize Es Penne. Xandie readied her salt bottle for a swing but dropped it as Es flamed the corpse. She lifted her salt-water bottle again when he continued to stumble toward the dragon teenager. Xandie squealed and flung the contents at the living-compromised man. The salt stuck and burned deeper than the dragon flames had.

The older man wobbled for a moment and then collapsed in a smoking pile at Es Penne's feet. She stared at the figure. "In the movies, when zombies get set on fire, they die. I guess real life isn't like a TV show." Es took off at a run toward her family.

"Sometimes I wonder about Point Muse. A

secret reality TV show would explain so much about this town." Xandie surveyed the battleground. Most of the mourners had fled, and the Braun family had enclosed the funeral home with barricades and salt. The owners of Elysian Fields were necromancers and were on the roof of the main building chanting. But they'd had little luck in controlling the dead so far. The cauldron controlled the dead, and until they salted it, the undead residents of Point Muse were funeral crashers.

"Xandie," Priss yelled and waved her over to the side of the building. "We took down half a dozen zombies, but they keep coming."

"When it's a cemetery, I guess they have the numbers. Is everyone okay?"

"Yeah, they're slow so we can avoid them. Most people left, except the necromancers, the dragons, and us. And the police are staying next to the barricades." Priss opened and closed a hand. "I wish I had my sword."

Xandie shuddered. "Wouldn't help. Then there'd be pieces still trying to eat us." She pointed to stray body parts moving on the grass. "Salt is the only thing that works. We need to salt the cauldron."

Priss nodded. "Right. Any idea where it is?"

"The last time I saw it, Archibald had it. So, wherever he is?" Xandie peered past the building. The Harrows had split up and were salting in different areas. Marjorie, Es, and Belle Penne were in one corner near the barricades, using flames to keep the walkers back from the car park. Ronald and Adelind holed up next to Archibald's bier.

Elspeth shrieked as she ran past, "Aieeee." She leaped onto the back of a walker and salted the man's head before shifting onto another body. "I see you, Marjorie Thistle. Don't think I don't know you stole my hair-loss recipe. I'm coming for you." Elspeth sang the last word and took off running, her late nemesis in her salt-killing sights.

Xandie sighed. "Elspeth's enjoying this way too much for a calm, peace-loving Harrow witch."

"I've got news for you. I don't think any of the Harrows are calm." Priss pointed to Xandie's cousins, flinging salt along with obscenities at the dead walking.

"I guess peace is overrated when you're trying to stop a mob of dead party crashers." Xandie pushed away from the building. "Come on, we have to find the cauldron." She figured zombie Archibald would stick to his family, his mom. All they had to do...

Priss interrupted Xandie's battle plan. "Look. Is that him?"

A lone figure shambled its way toward Adelind and Ronald Penne as they hid behind the wooden bier. The cauldron hung loose from the dead man's hand.

Xandie and Priss took off running, dodging any animated flesh that came their way.

Adelind screeched and flamed at Archibald. But he still mindlessly walked toward them. Moving away from Ronald, the dragon readied herself to transform, but Archibald only focused on Ronald.

"I thought he'd want to be with his mother. Why focus on his uncle?" Priss yelled at Xandie as they bolted toward the dragons.

"I have no clue. Whatever the reason, we need to get that cauldron."

Xandie sped up, puffing. She gasped words out between gulps of air. "I need to stop eating Lila's butter puffs." As she ran closer, Xandie heard Ronald yelling at Archibald.

"No, no. Not now. Stay back, Archibald." He produced a flame, but it weakened and sputtered before dying out.

Archibald focused on Ronald. A noise above

Ronald's head drew Xandie's gaze. Elspeth crawled commando style across Archibald's supposedly last resting place. Xandie grabbed Priss by the arm, pulling her to the side and out of range.

Ronald noticed and ranted at Xandie and Priss. "The great librarian and a dragon slayer afraid of a dead dragon?" He scoffed, and his face distorted as he continued to screech at them. "Help me. I'm a Penne, you have to help me."

Archibald's bland face rippled as he listened to Ronald's voice. His face jumped from non-responsive to enraged. He lunged at Ronald, but it looked like Elspeth would get there first.

With a cackle, she launched herself into the air and dropped a heavy octogenarian smack-down, right on top of Archibald and Ronald.

Ronald squealed and crawled out from underneath her and scrambled away. Archibald tried to follow, but Elspeth held him down and sat on his back. Elspeth flipped open the lid of her salt bottle and grabbed the cauldron from Archibald's loose grip. She whistled while she sprinkled salt onto the cauldron and swirled it around. Steam rose from the heated cauldron and over Archibald, spreading across the funeral home grounds.

Archibald shuddered and lay still, not a move made.

Xandie glanced around the cemetery. All the reanimated bodies had dropped, unmoving.

Elspeth clambered off the now permanently dead dragon and rubbed her hands in glee. "Right-oh. Dead people dealt with so who's up for barbecue ribs? I've got an appetite."

Holly sidled up to Xandie and gagged at Elspeth words. "I think she has witch dementia. There's something wrong with her."

Elspeth danced around the cauldron like a boxer winning a bout. "*Ha ha*. And you're related to me. Apple doesn't fall far from the tree, trust me."

Priss froze next to Xandie. Distracted from Elspeth's antics by the approach of the dragon matri-arch, Priss elbowed Xandie in the ribs.

"Oomph. Please, you bruise me, you feed me." Xandie shoved the elbow away and forced a smile on her face as Marjorie Penne approached them.

"Elspeth. I see it pays never to bet against the house," Marjorie drawled, a twinkle in her eyes, lighting up her dour features.

"Especially the way you play, Marjorie Penne." Elspeth took a swig from her flask.

"Give it a rest, old woman. The whole town knows, most of the time, it's filled with iced tea."

"The key phrase is *most of the time*. Who knows when that time actually is?" Elspeth winked. "Always keep them guessing, Penne."

Twin deputy brothers, Caleb and Riley Braun, strode over to the group.

Marjorie cataloged the Harrow girls, and glanced over Priss, then jerked her gaze back. A line formed on her forehead, and she cocked her head, staring at Priss. She opened and closed her mouth, puzzling over something. With a slow blink of heavy-lidded eyes, Marjorie Penne turned her attention to the police.

Xandie bit her lip. The brothers didn't look happy. In fact, they both looked green around the edges, and their sister, Melody, stood at the police cruiser, nibbling on a nail. Polish-mad Melody would never deface her manicured temple with a chipped or broken nail, let alone a nibbled one. Whatever was happening wasn't good.

"Mrs. Marjorie Penne?" Caleb asked the dowager dragon.

Marjorie arched an eyebrow. "I've known both of you since were born, Caleb Braun. You know who I am."

Caleb cleared his throat. He nodded to his twin brother, Riley, who produced a paper and read from it.

"Marjorie Penne, the Point Muse Police Department has a warrant to search your dragon hoard for multiple artifacts stolen from Point Muse residents. We have credible evidence that suggests they are at your residence. Officers have been dispatched already to execute said warrant. Here is your copy. Duly notarized by the parties involved. Thank you for your consideration and your cooperation." Riley let out a huge breath and extended the paper with a shaky hand to the dragon.

Marjorie reached out a hand tipped with shining silver claws. She speared the paper and read it before answering. "Then I suppose you should do your job, and I'll be there to make sure they discharge their duty." She bared her teeth and spun, taking Es with her.

Xandie watched Adelind and Belle trailed behind Marjorie as she sailed toward the car park. Of Ronald Penne, there was no sign.

The necromancer owners gestured to their gathered workers, including Holly, and started removing bodies.

The rest of the onlookers, the Harrows and Priss Makepeace, stared, shocked, at the police brothers.

"Are you crazy, Caleb Braun? Your mother will box your ears," Lila scoffed at the twins.

Elspeth shook her frizzy lavender hair, disgusted. "Marjorie Penne is not so stupid as to get caught by the fuzz. She'll open a can of dragon whoop ass on you, boy. Say your shifter prayers. Your brother can wipe up the mess when he gets back." Elspeth hoisted up her velvet cape and stormed away.

Xandie closed her still-open mouth. "What did Agatha say when you told her you were searching Marjorie Penne's place?"

"She told them they'd better get protection, and she apologized for dropping them on their heads as babies." Melody slunk up, chewed nails hidden behind her back.

"Like I told our dispatcher..." Caleb Braun frowned at his sister. "We have a credible witness statement that puts the artifacts in the Penne hoard, which sets up motive for Archibald Penne's murder."

"Oh. My. God." Lila threw up her hands. "She's his grandmother. Do you think her capable of killing family?"

Riley backed his brother. "Anyone's capable of murder. Just takes a second to snap. We have to follow every lead we find." He grabbed Caleb and pulled him away. Melody gave a wave to the Harrows and trotted behind her brothers.

"Zachy bear's gonna lose it with those two. I feel sorry for them. The Penne family holds grudges like nobody's dragon." Lila shook her head in shock.

"That isn't news to me." Priss shoved her blonde, curly hair into a bouncy cheerleader ponytail.

Es jogged back toward them, the rest of the clan absent from view. "Xandie, Grandmother wants you and your family to come up to the compound. She needs witnesses. And she wants to remind you of your obligations to the library and Point Muse."

Lila grabbed Xandie and Priss and towed them toward the car park where Elspeth stood waiting. "We're coming. I wouldn't miss this for a hundred butter puffs."

Xandie bit her lip. Was Ronald Penne right? Was Marjorie involved in the gallery fraud and the missing artifacts? And what had happened to the police finding the missing Iris Malone?

Finding Iris Malone was easy. Her crispy, fried body sat in the center of the Penne hoard, the art dealer's hand stuck to a missing artifact—the wish stone from the gift shop.

"It didn't help Iris," Xandie muttered in an aside to Lila.

"This town has gone murder happy since you arrived." Lila extended a foot and shoved a priceless gold plate out of the way. "I need to upgrade my serving-wear at the café. This gold stuff would look smashing against my food."

"Shouldn't we focus on the fact there's another dead body in front of us?"

"Come on, Xandie. It's a frame up. Marjorie Penne would never murder anyone herself. She'd have just ordered a hit." Lila choked on her spit when Marjorie Penne strode over to Xandie.

"Alexandra, you need to find out who did this. Who desecrated my hoard? Do this, and the Penne dragon clan owes you a favor." Marjorie swept a hand around the room. "And that's worth more than the gold in this room."

Xandie swallowed. "I'm not sure the police agree. The department will be as thorough as possible—"

Marjorie cut Xandie's words off with a slice of her hand. "We both know the boys are inexperienced. I've contacted the paranormal investigative group, and I'm trying to get in contact with Zachary Braun, but there're no guarantees he will be home before another person dies. You need to find the killer and clear my name."

Marjorie's stress was obvious. The dragon's smooth silver bob was in disarray. Hair stuck up every which way. Twin red spots on both cheeks burned along with the fire flickering in her eyes.

"And the great Marjorie Penne would never stoop so low as to hurt another person? Never cause pain or harm?" Priss hissed at her grandmother, anger in every line of her stiffened body.

Marjorie quirked an eyebrow at the stranger in her hoard room. "And you are? I don't believe I've ever encountered you before today."

"My name is Priscilla Makepeace, and it's your choice we don't know each other. You made your bed, now it's time you lay on it. Prison colors and all." Priss stormed out of the room, unable to hide her fury.

"Interesting friend you have there. I'd be more careful in the future who you depend on. She's a loose cannon." Marjorie weaved through the hoard like a graceful dancer until she joined her daughters and lawyer, Ronald Penne not in attendance this afternoon.

"Priss and Marjorie walk the same way when they're angry." Lila stared quizzically at Xandie. "What's the plan now that your main suspect is crispy?"

"Avoid Priss and Marjorie and stay alive."

Considering her track record for stumbling across dead bodies and killers, her chances were low on every count.

ELEVEN

"Xandie, some old weirdo's on the phone for you," Holly yelled over the top of Lila's lunch crowd.

Old weirdo? That could describe most of the over-sixty population of the town. Xandie took the phone from her cousin. "Xandie Meyers."

"You want the file or not, librarian?"

The troll investigator. She'd recognize that harsh smoker's voice anywhere. "It's paid for, I guess. It can't hurt." *Hopefully*.

"You want me to drop it off at your cousin's bakery?"

"Ah, no." Lila was the only Harrow aware of Sera's investigation. Xandie didn't want to upset the rest of the family. Especially Elspeth. Who knew where the radioactive hex fallout would land if her grandmother found out? And Theo wasn't having anything to do with the troll fiasco as he called it. "How about the small park next to Elysian Fields Funeral Home? It's more private."

"The dead center of town. I like your thinking, sweetheart. Thirty minutes. Time is money, so don't be late."

Xandie listened to the dial tone as the troll hung up on her again. Not one for small talk or social niceties. Then again, he *was* a troll.

"Everything okay?" Holly popped up next to Xandie.

"Yeah, just a library thing. I have to head out. Will you be okay with Lila's customers until she comes back?"

"Sure. I work here whenever Lila needs help, plus she brought in a fill-in baker for while she's at her dentist appointment." Holly ignored the customer waiting impatiently at the cash register. "She's dentist phobic, so they always give her something to calm down. She's a hoot afterward."

"Excuse me? I want to order now," the customer interrupted.

"In a minute," Holly trilled.

"This is unprofessional," the customer huffed.

Holly rolled her eyes and whispered to Xandie, "I caught Lila sneezing in a complaining customer's lunch once. Goddess knows how she stays in business." Holly pasted a fake smile on her face and turned to the woman at the counter. "Sorry. Important bakery business. How can I help you?"

Xandie turned away from the spluttering customer and slipped out the back of Lila's bakery.

Harrows were trouble magnets, but they were never boring.

———

Xandie adjusted her position on the rough wood seat. The Point Muse council had opened up a small parcel of land next to the Elysian Fields Funeral Home. Landscapers had turned the plot into a tranquil, picturesque garden for any family needing time after a loved one's funeral. Most days, it was a peaceful place to meet a cranky old troll gumshoe. Holly's bosses, twin sibling necromancers, had laid the walking dead residents of Point Muse to rest after the dragon funeral.

"Geez, you want to meet at a funeral home? You

witches have a death wish." The troll dropped onto the bench opposite Xandie with a long-suffering sigh. The seat groaned under his weight. "I heard about the zombie dragon incident. Nasty business."

She'd never met a troll in person. Barefoot, the private detective would have towered over an average sized man. He had muscled shoulders and tree-trunk-sized limbs. Hair was gray and coarse and close cropped in a military-style cut and his face was rugged, with large lines grooved into the skin around his mouth and eyes. She'd hazard a guess her gumshoe was a habitual frowner.

"I'm a librarian, not a witch. The death thing's my cousin, the banshee. This was the quietest private place I could think of."

The troll dropped the file he held with an ominous splat on the wooden table between them and smirked. "People are just dying to come here."

Xandie groaned. "Haven't heard that one. Is this my file?" She tapped the folder in front of her.

The investigator used a tobacco-stained finger to push the thick file over. "Here you go, sweetheart. The nitty gritty in print."

Bile rose in Xandie's throat, forcing her to take a quick swallow. She placed a trembling hand on top of it. "That's a thick file for a simple disappearance."

"Ain't no simple about it." He puffed his chest out. "Trollish Investigations is a full-service agency. In that file is a background check on all Meyers and Harrow family members." He lowered his voice. "That grandmother of yours, Elspeth. She's a scary one. Large parts of her life are blanked out; don't exist on paper, digital or magical. Her information's so redacted, it's just black paper."

"Elspeth's always been a tad shady in regard to her background." Xandie offered with a genuine smile. Her grandmother was mayhem incarnate, but she always had the Harrows' or Meyers' backs when necessary. As long as her grandmother had her bedazzled hip flask, the octogenarian was raring to go. "And the rest of the file?"

"Financial checks on both families, credit checks. Witch web and vehicle checks. Property and social media searches." The troll shook his head. "Witch-face, witchmention, and ask-a-witch had nothing on your mom but a bucket load on the rest of the Harrows." He shuddered, causing the table and bench seat to shake. "Your cousins' and aunts' photos should be illegal."

"Any other dark pasts I should know?"

"The Harrows have a few spotty arrests for protesting and sit-ins. A few for illicit substances and disturbing the peace. Just your normal run-of-the-mill witch family in Point Muse. But your mom's the interesting one."

Xandie drew her hand away from the folder, afraid to touch it in case the contents leaped out and bit her. "What's interesting about Miranda Harrow?"

"You could read it yourself."

"Or you could just give me the highlights, and I'll read it in peace later?" *Rip off the Band-aid, troll.* "My mom?" Xandie prodded the investigator back on track.

"I spoke to old neighbors of your mother. Both here and in Andrews, where she settled with your father."

"And?" Xandie didn't know whether the churning in her stomach was from suspense or the knowledge she was about to get more than she bargained for on her mother.

"Everyone loved her. Not a bad thing said. Except..." He trailed off and shuffled on his seat, looking everywhere but at Xandie.

"Spit it out."

"When your father left for work each day, your mother dropped you off at the neighbor's and picked you up just before he came home."

Xandie shook her head. "I don't remember that."

"The neighbor did. Full human and chatty. She made great cookies." The troll licked his lips at the memory.

"What was my mom doing while I was at the babysitter's?"

"That's the thing. There's no record anywhere of Miranda Harrow having a job during that time. No employment, banking, or tax records. Nada. Zip. And that's suspicious."

"How?"

"There had to be a digital or paper footprint. Did she have a coffee meet-up? Pay with credit? Did she meet someone for lunch and use her bankcard? There's no record of credit or bankcard usages during those blank times. Even human security cameras got nothing. I have a great tech witch who can hack, and she can find footage even from twenty years ago. But there's only a big blank. In my business, that ain't normal."

Her mother, even a mystery before she disappeared. "You have nothing on her?"

He scratched the side of his nose. "I wouldn't say that. Look, you gotta know. A twenty-year-old mystery is tough. Records were paper, not digital yet. And in magical departments, it's even worse. Supes are paranoid about security and more suspicious than humans. Getting answers is hard work. I went to an old contact of mine. He works in various projects for higher-ups."

"Higher-ups where?"

"Government, chickie. The human kind though, not supernatural. My contact did some digging and turned up your mom's name on deeply classified files."

"Has to be the wrong person. Mom never worked for the government." Mom had had no real powers, compared to those of her Harrow family, but she'd still grown up in a supernatural clan. Why would she have worked with humans?

"Your mom was a digger, as far as I can tell. She had a nose for crime, the super freaky woo-woo kind. Shadowy inner circle government types would call her in to consult. But my friend had to dig deep to even find that. The guy won't take my calls now." He grimaced.

"Are you saying my mother, Miranda Harrow, was a spy?"

"I'm saying she's murky like her mother. She wasn't all peaches and cream."

Xandie's heart fluttered, skipped a beat, then

pounded in her chest. "The knight confessed to chasing her off the cliff. What connection does he have to her death?"

The troll sighed and then looked Xandie straight in the face. "That's why I wanted you to read the file. So I didn't have to see you face to face." He took a deep breath. "I don't think your mother is dead."

Xandie reared back, his face tunneled in for a moment, hazed over with black fog. She shook her head. No way. Her mother was dead. Otherwise, why leave her only child? "No. The knight confessed to chasing her off a cliff. Miranda Harrow is dead."

"The knight chased her off a cliff and she fell, banged herself up good. But someone saw her fall. I got a real witness, one who swears your mother was alive after she fell."

"A witness?" Xandie screeched the last word, then took a shuddering breath in and let it go with a shrill whoosh. "Why didn't Point Muse police find the witness? What about the human coast guard? Surely, they would have found someone who saw my mother's death?"

"Nah, my witness is a merrow. A mermaid. They're secretive. No way she'd go near human police or coast guard. She told me she saw your mom fall, hit the water hard. The rocks banged her up so bad, the Mer assumed she was dead until your mom moved. The witness grabbed your mom and tried to return her to Wrecked Cove under the cliff Miranda Harrow fell off, but the tides wouldn't let her."

Xandie inched forward, on the edge of her seat. "What happened?"

"The fish dropped your mom off two towns over at their fishing port and never thought a thing about the incident until I came asking."

"My mom was only a few towns away?" All this time, her mother had only been a short distance away?

"The thing with merrows is they're flighty, with a short attention span. They have no sense of land or human map references. Her two towns over were a hundred miles away near Macon, up the coast."

"Mac... what?" She'd never heard of the town.

"Macon. Small town. Human with a few psychics. It's the eastern most point of the United States."

"Mom's alive?" Xandie's hands shook, and she slipped them under her jean-clad thighs.

"Twenty years ago, she was. I checked the hospital records, but they had a fire just after your mother arrived, and it destroyed the paper records."

"Convenient," Xandie mumbled to herself.

"It's not surprising in a small coastal town. It's the timing of the fire that concerns me. I had a look-see and talked to the residents. Most had no clue, but I found an old nurse from the hospital who remembered her. She said around that time, some fishermen found a Jane Doe near the harbor. The woman matches your mom's description."

"Why didn't my mother come home?" Xandie burst out, unable to hold her words back.

"Because of the head wound. The Jane Doe had no memory of her life before the fishermen found her. All the nurse could tell me is that a week after the cops made inquiries, black-suited government types swept in and took her away. The hospital was never told why the agents grabbed Jane Doe." The troll patted Xandie on the shoulder. "I'm sorry, chickie. The trail stops there."

"The government people my mom may or may not have worked for picked her up but didn't bring her back." Xandie leaned over the table, gritting her teeth and glaring at the investigator.

"Whoa there, librarian. Cover those pearly whites. I can keep looking. But even if they are humans, those shadowy government types cover their tracks."

Xandie closed her eyes, then forced them open again. Her mother's whereabouts had waited twenty years. The mystery could wait a little longer. The priority was Priss and a dead dragon. Even if Xandie didn't want it to be. She was the librarian and tough enough to focus on other things. "Keep an ear to the ground in case something bubbles up from your digging, but I have other bodies to deal with right now."

The troll slapped his hand on the picnic table. "Zombie dragons. Got it. I'll call you if I get any information. Then we can discuss my finder's fee."

She groaned; the library had paid one invoice, the next one was on her. She'd speak to Lila. Everyone in town passed through her bakery. Her cousin probably knew the witness and could set up a meeting.

"Check you later, library girl." The troll lumbered off, whistling a discordant tune.

She realized something. "Hey, you never told me your name," Xandie yelled after him.

He turned back and bowed to Xandie. "Herman Trollish, at your service."

"Your last name is Trollish, and you're a troll?"

"My mother was a traditionalist." Herman waved and stomped off.

"Interesting mother, Herman." She traced a pattern on the wood of the table.

Then again, what did she know about mothers?

TWELVE

Xandie navigated the stairs to her beach and the small dock. She hadn't wanted to deal with this right now but she felt like she didn't have a choice. She was here to meet with a woman named Coral Greenwater, who just happened to be the merrow witness to her mother's fall off the cliff. There was no doubt the mermaid had saved Miranda Harrow's life by plucking her from the ocean depths. The only catch was, by depositing her a hundred miles up the coast, no one had realized her mother had survived the fall. Coral had never breathed a word about it, preferring to stay off land-dweller radar.

The mermaids frequented her Aunt Amelia's veterinary practice because of their fish physiology, so Lila had asked around and turned up Coral

Greenwater. The mermaid had agreed to a meeting on Xandie's dock. Now all Xandie had to do was get to the beach without breaking her neck on the rickety stairs.

She flinched when one tread let out an ominous creak. "No more pastries, I swear," she promised the stairs.

"I'm not a pastry eater, but Lila's Chai Oyster chaser is to die for." A greenish, blonde-haired woman leaned the top half of her body on the dock and smiled.

Xandie exhaled as she cleared the last step and joined the woman. "Oysters aren't my thing." Xandie paused. "Ah, how do you..." She pointed to the mermaid's covered bottom half.

The mermaid flicked the tip of a shimmering emerald and lapis lazuli tail above the water. "We do a group order, and Lila delivers to the waterside for us. She's a full-service bakery. Caters to every supernatural." The mermaid shrugged, and Xandie glimpsed a pastel pink sports bra.

"Most land dwellers can't handle naked skin, so we found a great dive clothing company that designs clothing for us." The mermaid maneuvered backward and flashed her glittery bra.

Xandie cleared her throat. "That's great. I'm guessing you're Coral Greenwater?"

The merrow swam back to the dock. "Call me Cora. Lila mentioned you needed to talk about a swan?"

Swan? Avians weren't high on her interview list. "No, a woman who fell off a cliff twenty years ago. You fished her out and deposited her up the coast a hundred miles."

"That's what we call cliff divers—swans. But yeah, I was around the area, searching for new coral combs. She nearly took me out."

Xandie settled into a seated position on the dock. "That was my mother, Miranda Harrow."

"Oh." Cora opened and closed her mouth like a goldfish. "Glad I didn't leave her to drown."

"Can you tell me what happened?" What had happened to her mother after she'd fallen? Had she spoken to Cora? Had she mentioned Xandie?

"Once she'd sunk down to me, I snagged her and brought her back to the surface. The sea was rough, so I just went with the tide. Left her with some fishermen up the coast."

Where shadowy government agents had scooped up her amnesiac mother. "Did she say anything to you?"

Cora grimaced. "She was in and out most of the trip. She kept mumbling about her little girl, keeping her safe. I guess that was you?"

Xandie swallowed the golf-ball-sized lump that took up residence in her throat. "Yeah, that was me. Is there anything else you can tell me?"

Cora nibbled the end of her greenish hair. "It's probably nothing."

"Doesn't matter how small. Every piece of information helps."

"While I was looking for my combs, before your mother landed on me, there was a boat moored way out."

"What kind of boat?" Had someone been watching her mom as she fell off the cliff?

"Nothing fancy. But there were men in suits watching me. I thought they might help pick up your mom, but they just watched me through metal thingies."

Binoculars? Men in suits suggested government types. The same men her mom had worked for before her accident.

Cora shuddered. "I thought they might be big game fishers. Those killers are our boogeymen."

"What did they do?" Strange to realize mermaids had boogeymen. Xandie had spied the mermaid's very sharp teeth earlier when she'd smiled. The green-haired merrow would be a nasty predator when riled. What nightmare figure scared a vicious predator? *No one Xandie wanted to meet.*

"Nothing. They stayed back and followed us. I dropped your mom off at the harbor, and they stayed out. I noticed some of them left the boat and followed your mom once the fishermen found her."

The government agents who'd taken her mom from the hospital must have been watching Miranda Harrow. Somehow, they'd known the knight's plan. They'd been waiting below to snatch her. But Cora had derailed their plans, and they hadn't been willing to tangle with a mermaid. Could the government have been behind the knight's attack on her and her mom? Was the knight's plan to force her mother off a cliff into the waiting hands of the government?

"Sorry I can't tell you anything else." Cora pushed off the dock and floated. "Tell Lila we'll need an order for chasers tomorrow. We have a union meeting arranged."

"Wait." Xandie stood. There was one more thing she had to ask. "Was anyone around when my great-aunt drowned?"

Cora made a sad face. "Most of us were at our

annual conference in the Bahamas. Our queen was still here but couldn't get to Sera in time. All of us were sorry to see her go. She was a hoot."

"Thanks, Cora."

"Do you remember I used to brush your hair when you were little?"

"You did?" Xandie vaguely remembered Sera bringing her to the dock sometimes. But most of the time before her mother had disappeared was hazy.

"Sera brought you here sometimes, and she and my mother gossiped while I looked after you. You loved brushing my hair with my coral comb. Sometimes, I'd braid your hair. Normally you hated people touching it."

Xandie fingered her shoulder-length brown hair. Cora was right. She'd hated people touching her hair when she was a kid. Her mother had to bribe her to even sit at the hairdresser's. *Hang on...* "Did you give me a blue shell hair clip? It had gold glitter on it."

Cora clapped her hands above her head. "Yes! I had one, and you loved it. I gave one to Sera, and she sprinkled glitter over it for you."

Xandie smiled. "I still have that clip. For a while after Mom disappeared, it was the only thing I wanted every day. My dad had to take it away because it broke."

"It's nice to see you again, Xandie. So grown up and the librarian. Welcome home." Cora blew Xandie a kiss and flipped her tail up, diving and vanishing into the briny, deep ocean.

Xandie climbed back up the stairs toward the house and her cat, Theo. A mermaid had brushed her hair twenty years ago. Now here she was interviewing her about Xandie's amnesiac mother's rescue from death by drowning.

Funny how everything came back to Point Muse.

"Why do we have to meet here, Agatha?" Xandie held her breath. All the competing scents in the candle and soap shop 'All Lit Up' that her Aunt Winifred owned drove her sinuses crazy.

"Everyone knows I hate this girly stuff, and I'd never be caught dead here. If we want to keep this off the gossip rounds, we meet here." Aggie Braun's faded blue eyes bored into Xandie.

Xandie held up her hands in surrender.

Winifred broke in. "You want me to get your regular order ready, Aggie?"

Agatha nodded. "That would be great."

"I thought you wouldn't be caught dead here?"

"That's why she orders online, Alexandra. The Internet might be hit and miss here in Point Muse because of the ley lines but I've made sure my customers can order online with a special spell. Elspeth hooked me up." Winifred sniffed and shoved a brown paper bag at Xandie.

Xandie handed it off to Agatha. "What's so important you and I had to have a secret meeting in Aunt Win's shop?"

Agatha lowered her voice. "Marjorie had bail denied. They think that, because she's a dragon and rich, she's a flight risk."

Xandie snorted. "The woman's old. How far can her dragon wings take her?"

"Well, for now, nowhere. I've set her up as comfy as possible. But she ain't happy. She wanted me to remind you of your responsibilities."

What was that again? That's right...clear a dragon of murder, then said dragon owes you. Once again, she had to find a killer. *No big.* "I'm aware of my responsibility. Do the twins have any other evidence?"

"The twins don't. But I might. I was chatting to the old dragon and mentioned her daughter, Melinda. She got real upset when I told her there was a rumor she'd banished her. Marjorie denied it and refused to talk to me until Melody fetched her a mocha latte from Lila's. As far as she's concerned, her eldest ran away, and I believe her."

"Marjorie had no clue Melinda left because she thought she'd been banished? How was that even possible?" Was it the dragon dementia Ronald had mentioned? Xandie scratched at her arm, digging her nails in as she puzzled the problem. Ever since the rat infestation at Mayweather Inn, she'd had a damn rash on her arm. Maybe she should ask her Aunt Winifred for a potion to cure it.

"Look, Xandie, I might have an idea." Agatha made sure the shop was empty before continuing, "I don't want to undermine the boys and their job, but they don't have the experience Zach does. But I can't see that old dragon go to prison for a crime she didn't commit."

"And?"

"We need to dig into Melinda Penne's death. See what we can find out. I've got a feeling it's connected."

"What do we do?"

"I'll track down old Wolf. He was acting chief at the time of the accident. You can go have a chat with him. See what he remembers. He hates the Brauns and won't talk to us, but he might to you." Agatha gathered her parcel up and stuck it under a beefy arm. "I'll contact you when I have an address for him. And get that itch seen to. It looks like you've got a bug or the plague." Agatha nodded to Winifred and slipped out the shop door.

"I love Agatha, but sometimes those Brauns drive me crazy." Winifred slipped up next to Xandie and poked at the red, raised patch on her niece's arm. "Wowza. You have a nasty case of transferred dragon shale."

"Eww." Xandie drew back, horrified. "What's dragon shale?"

Winifred disappeared behind a counter and reappeared with a mortar and pestle and a handful of different ingredients. "Dragon shale is a rash caused by shedding a dragon scale and not looking after the exposed skin. Sometimes on rare occasions, once exposed areas become infected, the rash can be transmitted to humans. It's not common, but it happens."

Xandie rubbed her neck. The damn rash had started at her hand and traveled up her arm. It appeared straight after the rats showed up at Mayweather Inn. She'd assumed the gray vermin caused it. "A dragon gave me this?"

Winifred grabbed a few ingredients and threw them into a mortar and pestle, smashing them together. She hummed a discordant tune as she worked. Winifred nodded at Xandie. "Yep, a dragon caused it." She decanted the mix into a small bottle of clear liquid and gave a good shake before putting a stopper in the top. "All done. You need to apply this twice a day. You should be good in a week. I've only had to make this a few times. But I still carry the ingredients just in case. You're lucky."

"When was the last time you made it?"

"Oh, years ago. You were only a baby."

"Do you remember who you made it for and when?"

Winifred considered the question for a moment. "It was a long time ago, and Holly was still a baby, too. She was such a horrible sleeper back then. I was exhausted all the time. Elspeth threatened to mute her if she didn't stop screaming in the middle of the night."

"Was this around the time the crop duster crashed?"

"It could have been." Winifred nodded. "Yes, it was just after it crashed."

"Who needed it? The potion, I mean."

"A dragon?" Winifred chuckled at her joke. "One of the Pennes. That's all I can remember."

Winifred snapped fingers. "Hang on. Ronald picked it up for his wife. Does that help?"

Xandie nodded. It did if the original dragon scale shed was then used in a spell for dragon's breath by a crop duster to bring Melinda Penne down. The Penne clan declared her sister heir after Melinda left, and the ex-heir coming back threatened that position. And Xandie had touched Adelind's hair and neck, at the Inn during the rat incident. Maybe that's when she'd picked up the rash? If the dragon had a history of shedding a scale and getting an infection, then maybe Adelind *was* the killer. Xandie had only come into contact with four full dragons and only three before the rash appeared. *Adelind, Ronald, and Es Penne.* "Is that dragon shale thingy only a disease you see in older dragons, or can teenagers get it too?"

"Teenagers can contract it, but it's mature, adult dragons who are more susceptible. Teenage dragons have a super-charged immunity until they hit maturity so it's rarer."

So, not likely to be Es Penne. That left her parents.

"I'd keep wearing long sleeves while you have the rash. Just until it clears."

"Am I contagious?" Last thing she needed was to

give Point Muse a dragon-human plague. Residents would form an angry mob and run her out of town.

"No. Dragons can pass it to humans, but the contagion vector loses power once passed to a human. Not contagious, just not pretty. I'm sure Zachary Braun will be home soon, so you just cover up until it clears." Winifred winked at Xandie.

"Why is everyone trying to set me up with a mouthy, arrogant shifter?"

Winifred patted Xandie's arm—the opposite side to where the dragon shale rash had spread. "Because Lila and Holly are lost causes. You still have options." Winifred smiled and shoved Xandie out the door.

Xandie slipped the potion into a pocket. Harrows were hard-core. Chaos and mayhem were part of everyday life. Xandie smiled and scratched her arm. Harrows were family, but Zachary Braun wasn't. She'd avoid him when he made it back home.

"Hey, I texted you a few times." Priss hurried up to Xandie, phone in hand.

"Phones don't work so well here in Point Muse because of the ley lines. The energy messes with the signals. They only work occasionally or if you bribe Elspeth for a charm. I don't even bother to take mine out of the house half the time."

"Oh." Priss shoved the phone into her pocket and cleared her throat. "I wanted to apologize for losing it at the Penne compound. Going toe to toe with Penne villain number one wasn't what I had planned. Just saw red, I guess."

A temper, like every other Penne. Priss had inherited more than claws from her mother. "It's fine. An argument's what you get when two people with the same type of personality spend time with each other."

"I'm nothing like her." Priss glared at Xandie.

"You can shift claws, you both walk the same way when you're angry, and Agatha Braun's right. You have Marjorie's chin and her temper."

Priss took a deep breath. "Marjorie banished my mother. I guess the Penne clan is a sore spot for me."

Xandie weighed the information she'd gathered from Agatha and Winifred. Priss needed to know. "Marjorie didn't banish her."

"I have a letter. Trust me."

"Agatha spoke to Marjorie. She had no clue about the banishment. She thinks Melinda ran away. Agatha's good at spotting liars since her family's in law enforcement. Plus, Winifred had more details that helped. Marjorie's not the killer. Somebody else is."

Priss looked frustrated enough to sprout wings and fly away. "Then who is?"

Xandie headed off to Lila's bakery, with Priss following. "Let's get the girls and reconvene at my place with pizza for dinner. This might take a while to explain."

<hr>

"A chocolate and strawberry pizza. The food of the gourmet gods." Elspeth grinned and stepped inside Xandie's house.

"My eyes." Theo covered his and his pet imp's eyes, blinded by the glare that was the pizza delivery woman, Elspeth Harrow.

Elspeth did a shimmy and a shake, patting her fire-engine-red wig back into place.

Lila poked her head out of the lounge room. "What's taking so long, Xandie?" She opened and closed her mouth when she spotted her grand-mother. "Why are you delivering pizza?"

"Well, darling granddaughter, they had a job free, and I was bored. Plus, they let me decorate the uniform, and they gave me a moped for deliveries." She hooted and hollered and spun her green and red velour-bedazzled bottom in a booty shake.

Xandie copied Theo and covered her eyes. "The rhinestones cause temporary blindness and maybe insanity."

Elspeth sniffed. "Everyone's a critic. Now let's eat. You're my last delivery for the night and I'm hungry." Elspeth hauled a stack of pizzas into the lounge and dumped them on the coffee table. "Dig in."

Lila led a still myopic Xandie to the feast.

Priss and Holly opened the pizza boxes and dug in under Elspeth's benevolent and slightly wicked gaze.

"Do we have toppings other than chocolate?" Lila pawed through the boxes until she found a plain cheese.

Elspeth dumped her red and green Bros Santos jacket on the floor and grabbed her own slice. "Do you think I don't know my granddaughters? I even added in a special one for my freakish chocolate-addicted middle grandchild."

Xandie mumbled around a slice of chocolate and strawberry pizza. "Yeah. Thanks." She needed to cut back on the sugar in her diet but at the moment, the only way to keep up with the dead bodies and her Harrow family was with sugar-fueled adrenaline.

Theo shuddered and tore a small piece of meat

lover's pizza off for Horatio. "That addiction worries me. Anyone could buy her for a block of chocolate. And then what would I do with Horatio? Not everyone allows imps in their condos."

Xandie poked a chocolate-speckled tongue at her cat. "I'd be more worried about finding places that take talking cats."

Lila gave a timeout signal. "Can we please focus on the issues at hand? Namely, murder and dragons, instead of your conversation with your cat that no one else can hear?"

Holly and Priss waved Lila on.

"Right. Xandie found out information that might help us narrow our suspect pool and get Marjorie Penne out of jail." Lila bowed to Xandie. "Great librarian and nosy cousin, the floor is yours."

Xandie wiped her mouth for chocolate drool. "Agatha wanted a meeting at Winifred's shop. Turns out she's positive Marjorie didn't do it but needs evidence to show the twins before they can release the dragon. She's gonna track down a guy called old Wolf who was deputy chief of police when Melinda Penne died." Xandie paused, not sure how to word what else Agatha had told her. "She's sure Marjorie never banished Melinda. As far as Marjorie's concerned, your mother ran off."

"But the letter. It's from Marjorie, banishing her. It's proof she's lying. And if she lied about the letter, what else is she hiding?"

Elspeth grabbed a slice of pizza. "Yum, rhubarb, basil, and apple honey barbecue pizza. The Santos' make the best pizza." She stopped groaning when everyone looked at her. "What? I like this pizza. I can even take my teeth out to eat. It's perfect."

"I'm glad you're pleased with your denture-friendly pizza, but we're in the middle of something." Lila glared at Elspeth.

Holly choked on her mouthful and had to swig water. Eyes watering, she agreed with Lila. "What she said, just in a casual, non-confrontational, I don't want to upset Elspeth, kind of way."

"No fun. You're all so like your mothers. But Xandie's still my favorite. Besides, I've seen that letter young Makepeace is flashing around, and it's not Marjorie's writing."

Lila scoffed. "Please, you only want to be the center of attention."

Elspeth placed her pizza slice on the table and rifled through the small bag attached to her waist. She threw a wad of paper on the table. "Read it and weep, granddaughter. Lila Marie Harrow, I expect an apology." Elspeth crossed her arms and smirked.

Xandie and her cousins each grabbed a slip of paper. Priss peered over Xandie's shoulder as she read aloud.

"IOU, Elspeth Harrow. Signed, Marjorie Penne."

Lila held hers up. "Mine says the same."

Holly threw hers back on the table. "Mine is the same but adds that she owes you a foot rub."

Elspeth shuddered. "Like I'm letting scaly claws at my feet. Besides, she never pays up. The next hand, she wins them back. I kept these in case I have to blackmail her."

"Poker?" Xandie raised an eyebrow. Poker with the social elite of Point Muse. Not what she'd expected.

Priss ran a hand over the writing on Xandie's note. "My grandmother didn't banish my mom. Did she? We've had it wrong all these years."

Elspeth leaned forward. "No, sweetie. She hired investigators to find Melinda, but they never came up with anything."

"Did she know my mother was coming here to confront her when she died?"

"No. She had no clue your mother was the one hit by the crop duster. The paranormal investigator group and old Wolf kept the incident quiet. No one realized it involved a dragon. She had no clue Melinda was dead. Your grandma and your Aunt Belle were away on a trip. Adelind and Ronald were supposed to go but pulled out at the last minute because Adelind was sick."

Pulled out. Xandie ran the phrase through her head again. That, combined with the information Aunt Winifred had told her, sat in the pit of her stomach, already heavy with the pizza. "I know why they pulled out of the trip. Winifred told me the last time she supplied a cure for dragon shale was around the time of the crop duster incident."

"And?" Lila and Holly yelled at Xandie together.

"It was for Adelind, picked up by Ronald. And a core ingredient in dragon's breath poison is a dragon scale. If the crop duster sprayed dragon's breath, would it have been enough to take out a full dragon? Elspeth?"

Elspeth curled her lip. "Dirty poison to use. Hexes are so much cleaner. But yes, if the crop duster carried dragon's breath, it would have taken out Melinda."

"Bit of a coincidence that dragon's breath needs a dragon scale and Adelind had an infection from shedding a scale," Lila mused.

Holly rolled her eyes. "I don't believe in coincidences. But Adelind was the heir. Why risk it?"

Elspeth answered before Xandie. "She wouldn't have been the heir if Melinda had reached Marjorie. Marjorie adored her eldest child. Someone faked Marjorie's writing and banished her out of the picture. But when she came back, they had to do something more permanent so Adelind could stay heir."

"Is she capable of killing her sister?"

Elspeth snorted, pushing her teeth back in as they shot forward in her mirth. "She's a dragon. Of course she's capable. In fact, she's more likely to get her claws dirty than either Marjorie or Ronald. Her husband is a weak man who'd do whatever he's ordered to as long as he maintained his social profile within Point Muse."

"My dad said Ronald helped them leave Point Muse and gave them money from Adelind. The plan was to disappear for a while and wait for Marjorie to calm, but then Ronald turned up with the letter. It devastated Mom. She contacted Adelind after I was born. She wanted to change Marjorie's mind." Priss exhaled a shuddering breath.

"Adelind knew Melinda was coming back to town and couldn't risk the threat to her position. The dragon removed your mom from the picture so Adelind would still be the heir."

Priss stared, shattered, at Xandie as she processed her new friend's words. "Marjorie, my grandmother, never knew Mom died or that I was born. My aunt took everything away from me."

"And then you came back. She had to get rid of you. Archibald too, since you'd spoken to him. You're a target. Anyone who stands in the way of her remaining the heir is in danger." Xandie bit her lip, her chocolate cravings forgotten as she realized just what that meant.

They were all in danger.

THIRTEEN

"Whatever you do, don't touch the man's begonias. He's obsessed with them," Elspeth admonished Xandie and then ruined the caution when she fluffed her hair.

"This isn't a date. Agatha arranged the interview with the acting chief at the time of Melinda's death. We want information, not a love connection."

"I know that!" Elspeth huffed in offense. "We had a thing back in the day before your grandfather and Wolf's wife. I just want to show him what he missed out on."

Xandie rolled her eyes. "Revenge dating isn't on the list either." Anyone with information on Melinda's death, not the mating practices of octogenarian witches, would help. "What's his name?"

Elspeth shrugged. "We used to call him Wolf, and then old Wolf. But he's a hermit now. He's obsessed with begonias and grows the flowers in greenhouses. He lives up past Harrow house."

"So, that's the house?" Xandie pointed. At first glance, the small gray and white cottage with shingles was a picturesque Maine cottage. But if you looked closer, paint peeled off external walls, shingles sagged, the concrete path had a spider web of cracks in it, and the porch looked like a fire hazard. And begonias in pots covered every available inch.

"It is." Elspeth sighed and navigated the porch steps. "His wife died a few years back. The cottage has gotten a little rundown since." Elspeth banged on the door with a thump of her hand.

"I'm not interested in whatever you're selling. Leave me alone," a gravelly old man's voice rumbled from the other side of the door.

"Um, Elspeth? I don't think he wants to talk." Xandie backed up a step. Annoying a cranky wolf shifter hermit wasn't on her bucket list.

"Open up, you crusty old wolf. My granddaughter needs a word with you." Elspeth whispered to her hand and slammed it against the door. The cottage groaned and shuddered. But the door stayed shut.

"Look, Elspeth. Maybe we should do this another day?" Before he murdered them and planted flowers around their bodies.

"You've got plenty of potted begonias, Wolf. How about you have one less?" Elspeth grabbed a pot and swung. Potting mix sprayed the porch floor.

"Fine." The door swung open and a tall, grizzled, gray-haired man grabbed the pot from Elspeth and settled it on the porch. "What do you want?"

"Not me, old Wolf. My granddaughter, the librarian." Elspeth clicked her fingers at Xandie and then glared back at him.

Great, upset our one source of information. Thanks, Grandma. Xandie moved up next to Elspeth and extended a hand. Old Wolf stared at it, then at her. Xandie lowered her hand. "I'm the librarian. Sera Meyers was my great-aunt, and we need your help."

Old Wolf opened the door farther. "Well, why didn't you say that earlier?"

Elspeth stormed past the shifter and into the house without a word.

Xandie grimaced and followed her grandmother. Considering the unloved exterior, she dreaded seeing the inside.

Elspeth spun around in place and took in the

cottage interior. Every surface gleamed. Flowers gathered in vases and pots decorated the cottage in a blaze of color. "Old Wolf, it hasn't changed." Elspeth offered Wolf a sad smile. "She loved her flowers."

"That she did. I do my best inside, but I guess I'm not much bothered by the outside."

"She'd kick you for the peeling paint and then bake you a cake." Elspeth patted Wolf on the shoulder. "We need your help."

He sighed and hunched his shoulders. "You always had a one-track mind. No distracting you when you smell blood. Fine. Sit and tell me what you want."

Xandie perched on a cozy little chair in the corner of the room. The old shifter was like his house. Cranky, unloved exterior with a caring, warm center. You just had to dig for it.

"Well? Get on with it."

Elspeth stared at Xandie, encouraging her.

"We need to ask you about when you were acting chief. Around the time of the crop duster incident."

Wolf dropped into a chair and nodded. "I wondered when that would come back and bite me."

"What did you do, Wolf? I know that look. That's the *I got caught in dodgy business* look,"

Elspeth growled at her friend, sounding like a wolf herself.

"Gerald Braun was away. They called me in to be acting chief. A cakewalk, except Janie got diagnosed with cancer." He paused and swallowed. "It wasn't the best of times; she lost our first baby and then the cancer. I drank way too much, and the job suffered."

"The fire hydrant." Elspeth's face crumpled. "Why didn't you tell us?"

Wolf hung his head, shamefaced. "We were full of pride. Was our business, no one else's. Janie stayed with a sister in Portland for a while, but we couldn't afford the cancer treatment. Until the crop duster."

"Someone paid you to look the other way." Poor man, what a choice to make. Xandie couldn't imagine herself in that situation.

"A few days before the incident, someone contacted me, offered money if I looked the other way. We needed money for Janie's treatment, so I took it. I told her I'd gotten a raise because of the acting chief thing. She never questioned it."

"Who gave you money?" Xandie gritted her teeth, not willing to let the excitement build yet.

"I have my suspicions. But I couldn't refuse or

question. I accepted and drank more, creating a distraction by destroying fire hydrants."

Xandie probed. "There were never any names mentioned? Why they wanted you to turn a blind eye?"

"No, nothing. But then the crop duster happened. And I had my suspicions afterward."

Elspeth nodded. "It was horrible. Everyone was glad it wasn't worse. If the crop duster had dropped over town, it would have caused more damage."

"The damage it caused was bad enough. The pilot of the plane died and so did my friend's mother," Xandie chipped in.

"I got word the crop duster had crashed. I figured this is what they wanted me to cover up. We were understaffed, so I managed the crime scene, got the fire department in, but made sure they were friends of mine." Wolf licked his lips. He looked grateful to tell his story. "I found the pilot first. He'd ejected out, but the chute was damaged, and he didn't clear the blast zone in time. I expected to find debris, but everything burned hot and fast. Too hot for a crop duster crash. And then I found the dragon."

He faltered before continuing, "Found a mess of scales but little else. It wasn't a normal fire. Dragons are immune to fire, so I figured whoever paid me was a dragon rival taking out another one. I sanitized the area, doctored the books, and called in favors. The family of the crop duster got paid. You can check them out. There was never any mention of another body in the report, just the pilot. Then Braun came back, and the paranormal investigative group poked their heads in, and Janie started her treatments. No one spoke to me about the incident until today."

"Do you have the name of the pilot's family?" They might give her more to go on. Then Xandie thought of something else. "What did you do with the scales you found at the scene?"

Wolf stood and disappeared through a door before reappearing with a small, brown engraved chest. "The name of the family's inside. Along with this." He opened the chest, and a shimmering silver pink scale glowed.

"You kept it." Elspeth breathed the words out, transfixed by the glow.

"I cleaned it up. Couldn't stand to bury it. There's also a copy of the crop duster report in here. I figured the truth would come out, and the family of the dragon might want it." He offered the box to Xandie.

Xandie took hold of the open chest and stared at the scale. It pulsed, glowing brighter all the time.

"Xandie." Elspeth pointed to the necklace around Xandie's neck. The pendant was a gift from the library, passed from librarian to librarian over the centuries. A triangular pendant with an open eye inside the triangle shape with a rising sun behind it. The same necklace now blazed gold. The library wanted her to take the scale.

"Her family, her daughter, will want this. Thank you." Xandie closed the lid on the transfixing glow. "But you might need to head to ground. People are dying and it's to do with who this belongs to."

He shook his head. "Nope. Not hiding any more. My Janie's gone now, and she's the only one I'd worry about. The Pennes can come find me." Wolf stood, and the years and the weight of guilt poured away.

Elspeth cackled and clapped her hands. "About time, Wolfie. Let's plan your defenses while my Xandie deals with the scale. I have the best hexes available to you at only half the price."

That was her grandmother, always a deal to be made when it involved hexes.

Xandie nodded to Elspeth and Wolf and hefted up the chest.

It was time for Priss to have something belonging to her mother.

FOURTEEN

"Thanks for driving me, Priss."

"No worries. Besides, you gave me some of my mom back. And that's priceless." Priss kept one hand on the steering wheel and the other patted her chest where the scale rested on a necklace. "So, why don't you drive?"

"I never needed to in Andrews, the town I grew up in. When I worked in Portland, I never bothered having a car either. Plus, most Harrows have issues driving. Elspeth and Holly have scooters, and Lila has the bakery van she only uses for deliveries. But they're the only ones. Our powers react weirdly with engines."

"Fair enough. Who are we interviewing again?"

Xandie took a steadying breath. She wasn't sure

how her new friend would take the news. "Old Wolf told me the family of the pilot of the crop duster might have a name for us. Is that okay? Can you handle it?"

Knuckles gleamed white on the steering wheel before Priss loosened her grip. "I'll try. I guess I have more pent-up issues and emotions than I thought. But if it will get us a name, I'll shut up."

Xandie patted her friend on the arm for comfort. It was a start. Priss would heal, especially if Xandie got Marjorie off a murder rap, and then she'd meet her grandmother. Xandie checked the directions on her phone. Now that they'd left Point Muse, her cell phone was working again. "It's only two hours' drive along the highway, heading toward Portland, so we're almost there. The Mason Harbor turn-off should be our next off-ramp in a few minutes."

"Righto, boss." Priss waited for the off-ramp sign and steered the car off the highway. Ten minutes later, they were driving through the town of Mason Harbor.

Xandie pointed to a small gray detached cottage. "That's the place." The house might be small, but the garden was immaculate. Grass mowed, fresh flowerbeds prepared for planting. The house had a warm, homey look. Xandie stepped onto the front porch and rapped on the door. Priss hovered in the background. Xandie hoped her friend could keep calm enough for them to get a name or at least a solid clue on their villain.

A smiling silver-haired lady answered the door. "Can I help you?"

"I hope so. A man called Wolf gave us your name."

The woman's face paled, and she moved to close the door. Xandie slid a foot inside. "Please. We need your help. It's important. Life or death."

The older lady swung the door open. "Come in. I guess it's time to talk."

Xandie and Priss followed the woman into a cheerful yellow kitchen. The woman pulled out two chairs and motioned for the girls to sit. "Why did Wolf give you our name?"

"Because he wanted to help us. Help find a killer and bring them to justice. For everyone involved." Xandie gestured to Priss. "Her mother was the target. She was a baby when her mother died."

Priss nodded. "I'm not angry. Your family and Wolf were as much victims as my mother. I want the name of the person who planned the murder. Who's still killing right now. Can you help us?"

The lady opposite them covered her face for a

moment before dropping her hands. "The pilot was my eldest son, Ethan. My husband had just left us. We had no money, and I had no job prospects. Crop dusting was my husband's job. But when he left, Ethan took over." She paused, tearing. "He was in the army before. Wasn't right when he came back. We got this anonymous letter, telling us if my husband flew the crop duster into the indicated target, we'd get a lot of money."

"Why would anyone agree to killing themselves?" Xandie was equal parts horrified and pitying. To be in such a position to make that decision was a terrible predicament.

"The plane had a parachute. My son decided since he'd parachuted hundreds of jumps with the army, it wouldn't be a big thing to leap out of a crop duster. And then we'd have enough money to tide us over until I got a proper paying job. I had three other kids and a mortgage to consider." She wiped the tears away with the back of a hand. "I didn't want him to do it, but he wouldn't listen. Next thing, the police are knocking at my door, and the money's in our mailbox. He never made it out."

"Who hired him?" Priss pushed the lady, obviously hoping for a specific name.

"No names, but..." She paused, considering her

words. "The cops came first thing. The money appeared in our mailbox early that same evening. I was in the garage sorting things out. I didn't see the driver get out, but I saw the car leave."

"And?" Xandie let her voice trail off.

"The car was a silver BMW, and someone with long blonde hair was driving."

"You didn't see the license plate by any chance?"

For the first time, the woman smiled at Xandie. "It was easy to remember. PEN 1."

Blonde hair, silver BMW with the plate PEN 1? Sounded like Adelind Penne. It would be easy to mistake silver hair for blonde if you'd only had a quick glance.

The woman got up and reached behind a row of cooking books on a shelf. "Here. My son wanted to make sure his family didn't get into any trouble. He wrote a letter detailing everything. Plus, he kept the original note offering us the cash. You can take it. It might help."

Priss reached out and took the letters. "Thank you. This means a lot to us. To me."

The lady sniffed and stood, ushering Xandie and Priss out. "If you put away the person who arranged this, I'd appreciate it. Peace for my son and my family."

"We plan on it." Xandie grabbed the woman's hand and squeezed gently. "Thanks for being so honest with us."

The woman nodded and closed the door behind them.

The women walked back to the car, both silent, processing what they'd been told.

Priss pulled out of town and back onto the highway before she spoke. "Are you thinking Adelind Penne?"

"It's starting to add up. I'm not sure if Ronald knows and is covering for her or not. We still need to connect more dots. But yeah, I think the killer is Adelind. She's determined to be the only Penne heir."

"What's our next step?"

Xandie settled into her seat for the drive. "We get back to Point Muse and plan how to trap Adelind."

"That's something I can get behind." Priss flashed an excited smile at Xandie. Then she concentrated as they approached a narrower part of the road near the coast.

Xandie stared out the window, musing on the problem of the murderous Adelind Penne. She glanced over at Priss. Her new friend was handling the latest events much better than Xandie would have. Xandie frowned as Priss tensed, hands tightening on the wheel. She kept glancing at the rearview mirror and back over her shoulder. "What's wrong?"

"There's a car coming up fast behind us." Priss pulled closer to the edge of the road to allow more room for the car to pass, but the other vehicle stayed on their tail.

Xandie turned in her seat. The car was right behind them but she couldn't see who was driving because of the tinted windows. "Tell me it's not a silver BMW?"

"Nope. A green SUV. I can't see who's driving." Priss pushed her foot down, surging in front. "We need to get ahead and shake them. The road will open soon, and we don't want to go over the edge."

Xandie peered out the window. There was a ditch on her side. No coastline yet, but it wouldn't be too far away, not to mention more spots for a tragic accident to occur. Or in the case of Adelind Penne, an engineered accident, masking a murder. "What if we force them into a ditch? Take control?"

"They haven't done anything yet."

"That might not last for much longer. The SUV is on the move now." Xandie pointed as the other vehicle pulled up next to them and inched closer and closer to the side of their little blue car.

"Xandie, hang on. They're going to hit us."

The green SUV scraped the side of the car with a fingernails-on-a-blackboard screech of metal against metal.

Xandie hung on grimly as the little car bucked. Priss fought to keep them on the road. "Even if we ram him, would it make a difference since we're smaller than the SUV?"

"Maybe if we time it right. We might have a chance." Priss nodded to another car coming their way. "Hope you've got your seatbelt on."

Xandie braced herself for whatever her friend had planned.

The SUV must've spotted the car coming toward them and made a move to pull in behind them. Priss slammed her brakes on and hit the corner of the SUV, sending it into a tailspin. Then she sped off.

The vehicle stopped at a drunken angle across the road. The oncoming car sped past them and braked in front of the SUV. "Priss, you might just become my best friend."

"You only love me for my driving skills." Priss smiled at Xandie, a tad wobbly but faking composure.

Xandie shuddered. They'd come so close to disaster and only the quick thinking and defensive driving of Priss, plus lady luck, had saved them.

Adelind Penne wouldn't get away with murder again, at least not today.

FIFTEEN

"Let me get this straight. An unknown green SUV allegedly tried running your car off the road?" Caleb Braun ran a hand through his short, marine-style, sandy haircut.

Xandie cleared her throat and offered a tentative agreement. "Yes?"

"Do you have any proof this happened?"

"Uh, Caleb?" His twin brother, Riley, tried to interrupt.

Caleb held a hand up. "I'm five minutes older than you. I'm in charge, and I say quiet. I need to interrogate my witness."

"But you need to look..."

"Riley, give me five minutes here." Caleb forced a smile and continued. "Xandie, you and Ms. Makepeace were involved in an alleged vehicular incident. Did you stop and exchange details, call emergency services?"

Priss rolled her eyes. "They rammed us. No way would we get out of the car."

"Allegedly rammed."

"Caleb Aloysius Braun. You listen to your brother, or I'll box you around your ears and won't do your washing for a week." Agatha Braun stood in the doorway, glaring at her son.

"You whined to Mom? You should be ashamed of yourself."

Riley rolled his eyes. "And you should check out their car. A green vehicle has rammed it. Lots of paint scrapings left behind."

"Thank you, Deputy Braun, for your insight." Caleb heaved himself up. "You can fill out a statement when I come back in from checking your car." He stomped out of the station and gave his mother a wide berth.

Agatha Braun waved Riley off and stood next to Xandie and Priss. "Sorry, ladies. Zack's delayed, so Caleb's still in charge for at least another few days. I think I'll be grateful when his big brother's back."

Xandie wouldn't be happy to have chief cranky

back in town. "I wanted to thank you for setting things up for us with Wolf."

"Anything for you, Xandie. The old boy needed a shakeup, anyway. And I hear Elspeth is doing just that. Plus, setting up wards at his place." Agatha snickered and then sobered. "I heard you had trouble driving back into Point Muse today?"

"Someone rammed my car. Know any green SUV's?"

"Not personally, little dragon. There's a report taken this morning about an SUV stolen from the dragon compound." Agatha wiggled her eyebrows. "What's the bet it's green?"

Xandie shook her head. "I'll pass on that bet, thanks. Do you want to know what we found?"

Agatha pursed her lips. "You need to speak to Marjorie first. When you come back out, make a formal statement and present your evidence. But I think she needs to speak to her grandmother." Agatha nodded to Priss and pressed a button. "Go through to the holding cells. When you're done, buzz me. I'll let you out."

Priss stood, her face composed except for the thin line of her compressed lips. "Thanks, Mrs. Braun."

Agatha nodded and pointed to the door.

Xandie followed behind Priss into a different holding area from the one where she was incarcerated when the killer knight stalked her. Obviously, the matriarch of the Penne clan received more consideration than a lowly librarian did. She wasn't sure what to expect from this new area, but cheery yellow paint and white trim wasn't it. Holding Cell was stenciled in black ink over the top of the door. The central panel of the door was gray with a slot for food. The top and bottom panels were clear, though. What surprised Xandie the most was the fact the door was wide open.

"Hard times ain't hard with the doors open." Priss shot Xandie a frantic what-do-I-do stare.

Xandie rapped on the open door. "Up for visitors, Mrs. Penne?"

Marjorie Penne lifted her head and smiled at Xandie. "Alexandra. You've met my granddaughter, Esmeralda?"

Es sat cross-legged on a small silver and blue rug placed in the middle of Marjorie's cell. She met Xandie's confused glance with a grin. "I brought stuff from home to make it more comfortable. Gran posted bail but stayed here."

Marjorie raised a hand. "Peace, child. I decided

it was more peaceful here. Plus, once the killer acted again, it would be obvious I wasn't involved."

"As long as you didn't pay someone else to commit the crime to get you off the hook?" Priss smiled with her teeth, but it was a half-hearted effort.

"You have a terrible opinion of me, but yet I am at a loss as to why a stranger would care?" As Marjorie frowned at Priss, a considering look crossed her face. "Other than the last time you aired your opinion of me, have we met?"

Xandie reached out and gave her friend's hand a squeeze of encouragement.

"Not exactly." Priss took a deep breath and rushed the last few words out. "But you knew my mother, Melinda Penne."

Marjorie shook her head rhythmically. "No. No. My daughter Melinda had no family. She disappeared years ago."

"Twenty-four years ago, correct?"

"Yes." Marjorie's one word was closed, final.

"She was pregnant with me when she left town with my father, Simon Makepeace. He was a dragon slayer."

"I never knew his last name." Marjorie cleared her throat. "How is it possible you're Melinda's child? Dragons aren't compatible with humans."

Priss shrugged. "Nature finds a way. There are slayer records that mention hybrid births, but they're rare. I'm sure Xandie could dig up library records relating to the topic." Priss glanced at Xandie, who nodded agreement. "Plus, we think my father might've had latent dragon DNA."

"If that's true, why isn't my daughter here telling me this?" Marjorie eyes shimmered with unshed, iridescent tears.

Priss took out her mother's scale and passed it to Marjorie. "Not long after I was born, she tried to come back to tell you about me. A crop duster carrying dragon's breath hit her. Both my mother and the pilot died."

A single tear slid down Marjorie's face as she gripped the scale. "This was hers. I feel it. I was aware of the crop duster accident, but I was away at the time, and there was never any mention of a dragon involved."

Xandie broke in. The tension had built in the room, and even Es held her breath, waiting for the next development. "Someone paid the crop duster to target Melinda on purpose."

"But why? She left *me*. There was no reason to hurt her."

Xandie licked her lips, dreading what she had to

tell the elderly woman. She hoped the old dragon had a tough hide. "Melinda received a letter supposedly delivered from you, banishing her. Priss has it here. And a letter to the pilot of the plane offering money if he took the dragon out."

Priss held the letter out with a trembling hand to her grandmother.

Marjorie snatched the letters out of her hand and pored over them. She raised devastated eyes to the room. "This is not my writing. I would never banish her, and children are a blessing. Hybrid or not."

Priss swallowed. "That's not all. We have evidence either one or both, Adelind and Ronald, were behind it, and Archibald and Iris Malone's murders."

Marjorie reached out a hand to Es, both dragons shell-shocked. They huddled together, comforting and holding each other.

"Why do you think Mom and Dad were involved?"

"Because my Aunt Winifred sold a salve to treat dragon shale infection to Adelind at the same time as the crop duster incident. I contracted transferred dragon shale when the Inn was overrun by rats when I met with Ronald. Adelind was there too. Archibald was in a dragon art fraud scheme with

Iris Malone. He agreed to help Priss prove her claim, but he was killed, and the murderer framed Priss."

"Oh my gods." Marjorie collapsed against the cell bed, dragging Es with her. "After Melinda disappeared, I waited six months before I made Adelind heir. If I'd known Melinda had a child, I would never have done that."

Xandie walked up to Marjorie and crouched at her feet. "Ronald was a go-between. He delivered the letter, gave Melinda money, and she contacted him and Adelind when she wanted to meet with you. Penne-owned cars dropped off pay-off money. And someone tried to ram us off the road today. Coincidence? I doubt it. Someone doesn't want us investigating. I'm sorry, Marjorie, but the police have to know."

Marjorie's hand trembled as she gestured to a bottle of sparkling water sitting next to a hamper of food. Es passed the drink over, and Marjorie toyed with the open bottle. "Adelind's ruthless, but I never expected murder."

"Ronald met with me, and he implied you were losing it. Dragon dementia. And that you might be a silent partner with Iris and Archibald."

Marjorie snorted. "I have plenty of money, and if

I want to sell any artifacts, I can do it. No need to resort to criminal activities."

"He might've been the one informing the police too," Xandie offered, worried this might be the tipping point for Marjorie.

"Mom and Dad love high society. The parties, the respect and the fear everyone pays the Penne heir." Es rubbed her eyes. "I don't care. I guess I'm similar to my grandmother. Archibald and his mother are like Adelind and Ronald."

"Could your parents kill to keep their positions of power?" Priss's words tore a hole in the temporary peace of the cell.

"I would have said Mom would never have dirtied her hands and soul, but now…" Es trailed off, miserable. "My father follows orders. Doesn't have an autonomous bone in his body. He couldn't have thought this plan up. His whole married life has been about marriage to the Penne heir."

"Either one is capable of murder?"

Both dragons nodded. Es burst out of her seated position and paced the cell. "But Mom's concerned about Grandmother. She helped me get the hamper ready." She indicated the basket full of food and other items. "How could she do this?"

Marjorie calmed Es with a hand in the air. She

stood, an aged woman coming to terms with heart-break. Marjorie extended the scale to Priss. "This is yours. Your mother would have wanted you to have it." She smiled, a wavering curve to her lips. Es choked back a sob behind her.

Priss cradled the scale against her chest before slipping it back onto her necklace and hiding it away. She eyed Marjorie, as though uncertain what to do.

Marjorie made the first move and enveloped Priss in a tight dragon hug. "Welcome home, grand-daughter."

Tears ran down the dragons' faces.

After a while, Xandie coughed. "I'm sorry to interrupt, but we have to decide what to do next."

Marjorie dropped her arm and stepped back to the bed. "There's only one course of action." She glanced at Es. "I'm sorry, my darling, but the police have to know."

The teenager's face whitened, but she nodded her agreement.

Decision made, Marjorie sighed. Tension seeped away as she picked up the bottle of water and took a small sip.

Something niggled at the back of Xandie's mind, and her necklace warmed until it blazed against her skin. Adelind helped pack the gear for her grandmother, including the hamper and the bottle of water.

"Stop." Xandie rushed forward and slapped the bottle out of Marjorie's hand, but it was too late.

Es screamed as Marjorie convulsed, falling to the ground.

"Priss, get Agatha in here and call an ambulance."

Priss bolted for the buzzer and screamed for Agatha.

Es moaned and dropped to her knees next to her grandmother.

"Stay back." Xandie pushed her away. "If it's a poison fatal to dragons, it could hurt you."

Agatha and Riley slammed into the cell, first aid kit in hand. Caleb led Xandie and Es out and then collected the evidence while his mom and brother tended to Marjorie.

Priss stood in the doorway, arm around Es, both of them locked together in misery.

This was her fault. If Xandie had told Marjorie earlier, they might have stopped Adelind earlier. "I'm sorry, Priss. So damn sorry." Xandie stepped out of the way as ambulance personnel crowded the holding cell. The paramedics moved to stabilize Marjorie for transport.

Es elected to ride with Marjorie to the hospital in the ambulance.

As they passed, Priss shoved her evidence at Xandie. "Nail my aunt to the wall, Xandie." Her eyes overflowed as Es dragged Priss away.

Agatha came up behind Xandie and watched them load Marjorie into the ambulance. "That's what power and greed gets you. Twenty to life."

Xandie turned to Agatha and gave her the letters. "I want to make a statement on the murder of Melinda Penne, Archibald Penne, Iris Malone, and the attempted murder of Marjorie Penne."

Agatha Braun nodded and patted Xandie on the shoulder. "It'll be all right, Xandie. Marjorie's a tough old dragon."

Really? Because it looked to Xandie like the woman had lost a daughter, and her life, at the same time. And Priss would lose the family she'd only just found.

All because of greed.

SIXTEEN

The constant beeps of the life-support machine filled Xandie with equal parts relief and dread. Marjorie Penne had made it through the night but was in a medically induced coma. Thankfully, she'd only taken a sip of the poisoned water when Xandie knocked the bottle out of her hand. Priss and Es had stayed with their grandmother until the hospital had kicked them out to get some rest. Priss was staying with Es at the Penne compound.

"Any change?" Lila handed Xandie a hot chocolate from her bakery, and Holly placed two of Xandie's favorite pastries on a napkin.

"Thanks, guys." Xandie smiled and inhaled her hot chocolate. "No change. They have her in a medical coma, but she survived the night. Surprised everyone. Dragon's breath is deadly for dragons, but she only had a sip. The next twenty-four hours will decide what happens." Xandie broke her pastry in half. Her appetite had fled with her words.

"The police put a bulletin out on Adelind. She left in her car after dropping Es and the poisoned water off at the station. No one's heard from her since," Lila filled in Xandie. "Same with Ronald. The cops are worried Adelind did something to him."

"Priss and Es are under Melody's guard. She's ordering pizza in for them and will bring them back here after they've had food and rest," Holly offered in a quiet voice.

"And Mom, Winifred, and Elspeth are brewing potions and hexes in case of trouble." Lila rolled her eyes.

"I checked in on Theo and his imp, and they're fine. The library's on lockdown, and only Harrow blood can get in." Holly picked up a medical chart and flicked through. "Theo's worried and wanted me to let you know the library's concerned too. He said to be careful. He doesn't want to train another librarian, since your seasoning is coming along so well." She snickered.

"He's all feline heart." Xandie checked her

watch. "I'll find the doctor and have a chat about Marjorie."

Xandie closed the door to the dragon's hospital room. The tough old woman was *almost* as scary as Elspeth, but no one wanted to see the elder in a coma. Especially when her own daughter had caused it. A white-coated man with his head down walked past Marjorie's room, swerving at the last minute as he spotted Xandie.

Curious? Why did she feel she'd derailed his plan by standing in the doorway? "Excuse me, Doctor? Can I speak to you?" Maybe the anxious doctor had information on Marjorie?

The white-coated gentleman sped up and raced around the corner of the hallway.

"Hey you, wait." Xandie bolted after the man. She had a sneaky suspicion speedy Gonzalez wasn't a medical professional.

He disappeared through an emergency exit for the stairs. Xandie slammed into the heavy metal door as it shut in her face. "Ow."

She rubbed her nose and shoved the door open onto the deserted stairwell. "Great. Empty stairs leading to a deserted parking garage. That doesn't scream horror movie at all."

Taking a deep breath and steeling her nerve,

Xandie followed the trail of discarded clothing into an underground garage. She toed a doctor's white coat out of the way. "Freaky striptease." She shoved the doors to the garage open and stumbled over a stethoscope. Xandie hissed as she landed on her knees on the bare concrete. Thank god she'd worn jeans today. Otherwise, Theo would tease her about grazed knees.

"Coordination doesn't run in your family, does it?"

Scrambling back, Xandie pushed herself upright. An older man with a gray, military style haircut and a plain black suit frowned at her.

"Excuse me?" Perfect strangers should keep their comments on her lack of athletic ability to themselves.

"It's the age-old argument of nature over nurture." The older man lit a cigarette, ignoring the no smoking sign overhead. "If you'd had your mother for longer than five years, would you have been as agile and adept as she is? It's an interesting debate."

He was talking about her mother like he knew her. But how? Who was he? Only one way to find out. "How do you know my mother died when I was five?" Dying, disappearing, amnesia—same thing to a five-year-old.

Guffawing, he snuffed out his cigarette with a thumb and a finger. "We call it actively recruiting. Your mother, injured or not, was an asset."

"You're the government men my mother worked for before she disappeared."

"And afterward."

He beamed a smile at her the way a pet owner did when their doggie performed a trick. She fought a shiver. Anyone who treated a person like an animal wasn't someone she wanted to associate with.

"As I said, a memory isn't needed. Your mother's skills as an investigator and catalyst are innate and second to none. We weren't going to let that talent go to waste."

Waste? He'd stolen her injured mother away from a traumatized child. "You're a monster. I was five. I needed my mom," Xandie yelled, heart pumping a staccato beat. Her necklace blazed hot, a burning, circular brand. Xandie spotted a tiny, shadowy figure scooting past the plain, nondescript, government issue vehicle. Had the library sent a rescue party?

"I'm pure human. Not a monster, like those you surround yourself with. Your country needed your mother more than you did. You have no clue the fight your fellow Americans are involved in against supernatural cabals. Their corruption influences the very foundations of your society. Your mother, before her incident, was an important asset. Close, intimate knowledge of the supernatural world with no ostensible powers or supernaturally disfiguring features. Once unburdened of her family and supernatural memories, she became perfect for our use."

Perfect? What crazy Kool-Aid was this guy guzzling?

A skittering of nails under the government car had Xandie twitching. She shifted her gaze away, not willing to draw attention to what could be the library's escape plan. "You're psychotic. Where is my mom?"

The unnamed agent grimaced. "That's the problem. She disappeared. We've been trying to track her for the last seven years. She's at the top of our most wanted list now because of her knowledge of our inner workings."

Xandie bent over, great peals of laughter ending in a snort ripped out of her. "Oh, that's classic. You stole her then lost her."

Half a dozen more knee-high shadows joined the other one under the agent's car.

"I thought you would appreciate the irony. And that's why you'll help bring your mother in."

When Hell froze. "Nope. Not happening."

He raised a fist, and two more black-suited men stepped out, weapons drawn. The older man pointed his own weapon at Xandie. "You don't have a choice."

Shadowy critters swarmed the agent's car, gray-green leathery skin blending to camouflage with the vehicle. Metallic popping noises echoed in the empty garage as screws and bolts exploded out of the car. Panels dropped off and doors hung drunkenly.

The two younger men threw their guns away as the creatures swarmed and climbed their arms and legs.

The agent in front of Xandie swung his legs as the leathery goblins clamped sharp claws onto them. With a curse, he threw his gun, and a group of her rescuers jumped on it, screeching and howling until they reduced the weapon to bits and pieces. One animal let out a satisfied burp, before rolling over and patting his gray tummy.

Xandie smirked. "Never bring a gun to a super-natural fight. You'll lose every time."

"One way or another, you'll lead us to your mother." He grunted, trying to twist and move arms now pinned to his sides by the gremlins hugging him.

"I won't. Wherever I go or whatever I do, the

library will protect me. And I'm sure that goes for my family, absent or otherwise. If you don't want an all-out supernatural war, you'd better stay out of Point Muse and my life."

"You should listen to the little librarian." A tall, muscled man with a shock of blond hair stepped up next to Xandie.

More library help? "Yeah, what he said." Xandie poked a finger at her new ally.

"We'll never stop watching her. Miranda Harrow *will* come re-join our task force," the agent spat, his face glowing red as he twisted.

Other muscular men, with varying shades of blond hair, surrounded the agent and his men.

"Look, but no touch, human." Xandie's new ally sneered at the prisoner. "I'd stop struggling, or those kobolds might forget they eat metal and start devouring flesh."

He ceased his movements, eyes wide.

Bowing to Xandie, her ally gestured to the government agent. "With your permission, my men will deliver these gentlemen back to their employers."

She got the impression her new friend knew who her black-suited enemies were. "And their employers are?"

The blond man grinned, his front teeth pointed. Smoke trickled from a nostril. "The American government has not always been so inclusive of different races and species. These agents' task force, the Anti-Species Project, has been in place, deep in the government's core since the fifties. Originally funded by the Pura Sanguis." He cocked an eyebrow. "I gather you've had run-ins with the pure blood knights?"

Xandie wrinkled her nose. "Unfortunately. Hang on... Anti-Species Project. ASP? They work for a task force that has the acronym ASP?"

Her ally shrugged. "Humans aren't that imaginative. We will return him to his bosses. They won't try a face-to-face meeting again for a while now that they've tested your defenses." He flicked his fingers, and his men dragged the agents away.

"Hey," Xandie protested. "He had information on my mother."

"They might hate the supernatural, but they aren't above forcing those with powers to barricade their minds. Even in interrogation, their minds are impenetrable. He wouldn't have given you any more information."

"I take it you've come across these guys before?"

He grinned, shark teeth on display. "Once or twice."

Xandie bet her new ally had come out on top of every encounter. The predator vibe was strong in this one. She stuck her hand out and introduced herself. "I'm Xandie Meyers. Thanks for the assist."

"Ladon. I'm a Hesper Gold. The library knew we'd tangled with ASP before, so it called for help."

Hesper Gold? She hadn't come across that supernatural species in her research yet.

Taking pity on her confusion, he explained, "We are golden dragons who guard the garden of Hesperides and the golden apples of immortality."

"Is that the garden that has nymphs and belongs to the Greek Goddess Hera?" At least she didn't look completely ignorant, that much information she knew.

"The nymphs vacated when Hera moved us in. We were heading to Point Muse Hospital when the library sent out her distress call."

"Why the hospital here?" There had to be closer dragon hospitals they could go visit.

Ladon smiled, with teeth covered, and held up a golden-stoppered bottle. He cradled it in his hands. "A long time ago, when the matriarch was young and impulsive, she saved the life of a Hester child. He protected his apple tree against thieves, and Marjorie leaped to his defense. We're returning that favor." He extended the bottle to Xandie. "This will heal her from her unending sleep."

Xandie received the prized bottle. "Won't this make her immortal?"

"Dragons are long-lived already, and this is a small dose."

"Thank you. The Penne clan will appreciate this."

He winked. "We'll see. Marjorie is formidable although your Elspeth's reputation precedes her. We'll see you again, librarian." He turned to go.

"Uh, Ladon? Your little gremlin friends?"

"Of course." He snapped his fingers, and the kobolds swarmed out of the garage. With a tip of his head, the gold dragon followed them.

Cradling the bottle, she took a sharp breath and headed into the hospital. This immortal elixir would help heal Marjorie, and then they could track down her attacker, Adelind, and clear Priss's name.

Xandie reached the hospital room, surprising the doctor and her cousins.

"Where have you been? The doctor's updating us on Marjorie's condition." Lila reclined on a chair close to the dragon's bed.

Holly turned from reading the chart. "She's not responding."

"I can help with that." Xandie held up the golden potion.

Gasping, the doctor pointed. "Is that what I think it is?"

"If you think it's a gift made of immortal apples given to me by a golden dragon, you'd be right."

"This will bring her out of her coma, and being a dragon, she'll suffer no secondary complications. We'll get this administered."

Xandie deposited the bottle into the doctor's waiting hands and gave a sigh of relief as he disappeared with the babbling nurses in tow.

"And will you inform us how you got hold of an immortality potion?" Holly squinted at Xandie. "Why are you mussed?"

"Fighting with dead bodies, probably." Lila smirked.

"Happy to divulge details. But I need to check on Priss and Es first. Can someone run me out to the compound?"

Holly jiggled her moped keys. "Take a walk on the banshee side. You'll never go back to riding in a bakery van again."

Lila poked her tongue out at her cousin. "I'll wait

here until you get back. Try to survive Holly's driving. Like Theo, I don't want to break in another cousin."

Nose in the air, Holly ignored both her cousins' laughter as she sailed out of the hospital room.

SEVENTEEN

Xandie waved as her cousin zoomed off on her silver moped. Considering Holly was the quiet cousin, Xandie expected her to be a sedate driver. Except she wasn't... Xandie shuddered at the image of the poor dog leaping out of their way into a ditch when Holly had gone off-road to avoid traffic. Hopefully it wasn't a shifter otherwise the Harrows would be hauled to the station in a heartbeat.

Nodding to the guard at the front of the compound, Xandie stepped through the gate as it opened. The house stood out from the groomed landscape surrounding it. Dark red and brown brick frame, with white columns and trim around the windows, made the building look inviting instead of an ostentatious outpouring of dragon wealth. Xandie paid little attention when she'd been here with the police, searching the hoard and finding Iris Malone's body.

She passed Deputy Braun's police cruiser. Melody was here in case Adelind circled back to the compound. It would destroy Marjorie if she woke from the coma to find Priss or Es missing or hurt.

Pressing the buzzer, Xandie waited for someone to answer. Five minutes later, she was still waiting. She pushed the buzzer again, but the door didn't open. Frowning, she tried the handle, and it turned with a quiet click. Where were Melody, Priss, and Es? Even watching a movie and eating pizza, they should have heard the doorbell. Xandie tried to phone Priss but got no dial tone. Point Muse ley lines had struck again.

"Melody? Priss? Anyone there?" Xandie stepped inside. What were the odds the three girls hadn't heard her? "Pretty damn low," she whispered to herself.

Creeping forward, she peered into an empty study, then kept moving through the house. The bathroom and the front receiving room looked likewise empty. Xandie opened the kitchen door and stumbled over the inert body of Deputy Braun.

"Melody." Dropping to her knees, Xandie felt for

a pulse. She sagged as the slow beat registered under her fingertips. Xandie turned the shifter's head and ran her palm over a large lump and small cut at the base of her skull. The deputy should be okay, but Xandie needed to find Priss and Es. Hopefully intact. "Don't worry, Melody. I'll handle it."

Xandie spotted another door off the kitchen, but it was only an empty butler's pantry. A line of sharp knives mounted on the wall snagged Xandie's attention, and she grabbed a small paring knife. Now where would a teenager eat pizza and watch a movie? A thump overhead froze Xandie in place. *Her bedroom, that's where a teenage dragon would feel safe.*

Heading out the way she'd come in, Xandie raced up the stairs. Once she hit the first floor, the rooms were empty of life.

Xandie paused at a door; this one had a cartoon of a dragon and St. George pasted across the front. Odds-on favorite this room belonged to a teenage dragon. She peered in. A few pizza boxes upended with contents strewn across the floor. Pillows and cushions scattered across every available space and one of Priss's beloved swords snapped in half and bloodied on the end.

Holding her breath, Xandie crept inside and grabbed the hilt end of the sword. Even broken, she stood a better chance against an enraged psycho dragon than without a sword.

A thump from a room to her left grabbed Xandie's attention. She held the shattered sword up high and kicked the door wide.

Es Penne lay trussed up on the floor of the bathroom, gagged. Her black and silver hair was disheveled and frazzled. Flipping her hair back, she stared at Xandie with wild eyes. Es drummed her feet on the floor and opened her eyes wide.

Holding her sword-free hand out, Xandie tried to soothe the terrified girl. "It's okay. I'll get you out of here, but just stay calm."

Es grunted behind her gag.

Xandie kneeled next to Es and sawed at the rope around the teenager's hands with the half sword. "It's okay. I found the deputy. She's breathing. Don't worry about your…"

Her words trailed off as Es stiffened, fear and bitter hate in every line of the teenager's body. Xandie started to turn as a heavy clawed hand came down on the back of her head.

As she collapsed, Xandie spotted Es sliding the

sword behind her as the bathroom darkened away to black.

At least one of them might get out of here alive.

Jagged lightning split Xandie's head as she rolled over onto her side. "Hangover hell without the benefit of a foggy memory and good vibrations." She grunted when a rock dug into her bottom. *Rock?*

Xandie eased her eyes open, expecting to see the white, glossy tiles of Es Penne's bathroom, but instead, there was a rough granite ceiling above her, and sand and rocks surrounded her.

"Caves near your library. In case you're wondering?"

It shamed her to admit it, but the sound of her friend's voice was as good as chocolate. "Priss?" Xandie squinted and made out the vague figure of someone else slumped against the opposite wall.

"Alive and tied."

"I found Melody. She's out cold and bleeding."

"Yeah, she got hit first. I went down next."

Xandie pushed herself to a seated position. She leaned back against the rough wall. "I found Es, almost freed her until Adelind knocked me out."

"About that…" Priss sounded embarrassed.

"Where *is* Es? She was trying to tell me something, then Adelind bopped me on the head." Xandie hadn't been quick enough to free Es, but with the broken sword, she was sure the resourceful teenager would do it for herself. *And lead the rescue party straight to them.*

"Es isn't here. I assume the killer left her. I don't think they wanted her harmed."

"At the very least, that's something in Adelind's favor."

"That's the thing. We made a tiny miscalculation."

"About Adelind?"

"It wasn't her who hit us. It was Ronald."

Say what? She'd pegged Ronald as a follower, not a doer. "Carrying out his wife's orders. Right?"

"This is all Ronald, darling. Do you think I'd poison my mother?" Adelind's disgusted tones echoed through the cave.

"Adelind?"

"Yes, Adelind. The Penne heir, mother of Esmeralda, wife to a murderer. The gossips will milk this atrocious story for all it's worth."

"Let me guess. Ronald banged you on the head, tied you up, and left you in a cave?"

"Smart librarian. Yes, I left this morning for my spa appointment. Next thing I know, Ronald pops up wearing a blond wig and I wake up in this filthy cave of unwanted discards."

"He pretended to be the pizza boy and took Melody out, then me. I woke up here to my aunt's vengeful tirade against her no-good husband."

"Don't call me that. I have no proof you're Melinda's child, and I don't believe Ronald would kill my sister."

"Oh, he did. The police have the proof. Marjorie's seen the letters. She believes Priss is her granddaughter."

There was dead silence for a moment as Adelind digested the news. "Is my mother alive?" she asked.

Beneath the anger, Xandie heard her desperate grief hiding.

"Yes, Alexandra. Is my mother-in-law alive?" Ronald Penne's plummy tones filled the cave.

Xandie closed her eyes and whispered to the library to send help. Her necklace tightened for a second and then released. A sharp shape underneath her bottom poked her tender skin. *A knife*, the same knife she'd removed from the butler's pantry.

"Well?"

Xandie forced herself to sound grief stricken.

"She…I'm sorry. Marjorie passed away before I left for the Penne house. I wanted to break the news myself." If Ronald thought Marjorie was dead, he wouldn't try to hurt the elderly dragon again.

"Oh God." Adelind choked off a cry, falling silent.

"Damn you," Priss cursed. "What next, Ronald?"

"Well, darling niece, since Marjorie's dead, I kill you. And my sweet wife must go, as she's the current heir, and I'll take over as regent until Esmeralda's of age."

"Have you met your daughter? No way will she allow someone else to be her mouthpiece." Xandie snickered at Es following orders.

"I'm her father. She'll do as I tell her." Ronald puffed his chest out. He extended a sharp dragon claw toward Xandie. "As for you, I have no fight with the library, if you keep your trap shut. I'll bring a forget-me-witch to wipe your memory and release you."

Xandie shuddered. She had no clue what kind of witch that was, but it sounded vaguely familiar, like she'd heard the term in passing somewhere before. Still, the thought of letting one near her gave her the heebie-jeebies.

"And Priss and Adelind? What are you going to do to them?"

"I've found an appropriate way to dispose of my family issues." Ronald's smile widened. "I am, by far, the best choice to take the clan forward into a glorious drakon future."

"Wow, Adelind. You married a nutcase." Xandie couldn't believe the tripe Ronald was dribbling.

"He was desperate for a powerful dragon name. When I married him, I thought he'd be an asset to the clan." Adelind sniffed.

Priss snorted. "More like you thought he'd do whatever you wanted."

Adelind snapped at her niece, "It's not my fault. He's mentally defective."

Compassion was *not* Adelind's middle name. Xandie wriggled and winced when the blade jabbed into skin. She shifted to see if she could touch the blade, but her hands were tied, and the knife wasn't hidden between her clothing any longer but wedged between her back and the wall. It must have fallen out of her clothing when the dastardly dragon dumped her on the ground.

"Now, now, librarian. No point wrestling against my ropes. I'm brilliant at knot tying." He waggled a finger at Adelind. "And sorry, darling, but the ropes are spelled. You can't flame them or slice them with your claws. Sit tight until I return with the witch."

"What about Priss and Adelind? You haven't told me how you'll kill them." Xandie kept him talking. Her cousins would realize she was in trouble when she didn't call. She hoped Es knew where her father had taken his victims. Because otherwise, who would check in a deserted cave underneath her house?

"Why, drown them, of course." Ronald looked confused, as if he expected more from Xandie. "Adelind is a fire dragon, so she can't breathe underwater, and Melinda's child is a hybrid. No powers to speak of. All my loose ends dealt with and no messy bodies to dispose of. I'll bring the witch here and then release you. Hopefully before the tide comes in." Ronald winked and blew a kiss to his soon-to-be-dead wife. He disappeared through the mouth of the cave.

"Aunt, I hope you had a prenup in place. If you escape, you'll need it."

Adelind growled. "We're dragons. Of course I did."

"I lied. Marjorie was alive when I left. The

doctors expect a full recovery once they administer a special antidote for the poison.”

“There is no antidote for dragon's breath,” she replied bitterly. “No matter what the doctors do, my mother will die. The poison has a one hundred percent kill rate.”

“The immortality potion a golden dragon gave me for your mom might help.”

“The Hesper dragons came to my mother's aid? Why? What did she have on them?”

“She saved a young Hesper dragon years ago. They're just repaying the favor. She'll be fine, but right now, we aren't. Es grabbed the broken sword, so I'm hoping she's escaped by now and notified the cops.”

Adelind whispered her thanks.

Xandie wriggled until she grasped the knife underneath her. Ronald had tied her hands behind her, which made grabbing the blade much easier.

“Xandie? You're quiet. Are you okay?” Priss rolled across the uneven ground until she faced Xandie.

“Just trying to reach the knife I hid so both of you can get rid of your ropes.” Xandie rolled against the wall and levered herself to her knees. She shuffled forward, knife gripped tightly and teeth gritted as sharp rocks cut into her jeans-clad knees.

She let out a squeal as she toppled into an indentation in the sand. After wriggling around, she managed to flop onto her side. Xandie flipped the knife toward Priss, but it landed near Adelind instead. "That's the best I can do. Any of you reach it?"

"No chance unless I wriggle like a worm on a hook. What about you, Auntie?"

Adelind sat up and used her feet to push herself forward. She reached the knife and pulled it toward her with her feet. She grunted as the sharp edge nicked skin. "Don't call me Auntie."

She braced the blade against a rock and rubbed her bound hands up and down until the ropes fell away. Adelind undid her bound ankles and stretched. She turned to cut her niece's bindings, but rocks falling outside and raised voices froze her.

"Quick, give Priss the knife. And get out of here. One of us needs to lead the cops here," Xandie hissed at the dragon.

Priss snatched the blade from her aunt. "Escape while you can."

"That ex-husband of mine will regret his actions

for the rest of his short, miserable life." With that, she slunk out of the cave mouth and disappeared.

"Hurry."

"What about you?" Priss sawed at the ropes on her wrists.

"He won't kill me. I just get a memory wipe. You need to leave before he comes back."

"Too late." A figure leaned over Xandie. Ronald's face contorted with rage. "How did my annoyingly alive wife escape?"

"Maybe the ropes weren't dragon proof." Xandie shrugged, unconcerned.

Ronald leaned over Xandie and yelled, spit spraying over her, "I will track her down. I will be the heir." Ronald grabbed Xandie by an arm and dragged her over to Priss. "Someone snuck in a knife. How practical."

He grabbed the knife from Priss and sneered at her attempts to escape. "One of you dead is better than nothing." Ronald kicked Priss in the side and tapped his foot in a small puddle of water that had filled while he'd been talking. "Few minutes more and this cave will fill, and you'll be out of my hair."

Priss smiled. "I'm glad I'm not slumming in your gene pool."

Ronald screamed at her defiance and dragged

Xandie to the beach outside. "Climb. The witch is at the top. He's under orders to hex you if you do anything but climb."

"Hard to climb with hands and feet tied." She hopped on the spot to emphasize her point.

Ronald pulled his perfect non-moving hair and grew a claw and sliced the ropes securing her ankles and wrists.

Moving to the rock face, Xandie waited for Ronald to join her, but he moved back to watch as the sea rushed in. She grabbed a hunk of granite and hauled herself up as the incoming tide covered their footprints in the sand. Another large wave surged inside the cavern. Xandie hung off the cliff face, waiting for Priss. She sagged when no one appeared.

"I knew my plan was foolproof." Ronald clapped like a child and glared at Xandie. "Keep climbing, unless you want to join my niece in her watery grave."

Choking back sobs, she climbed as fast as her lack of athleticism allowed. Hands stretching for holds, she scrabbled to cling to the rocks. Xandie had no clue how long the climb had taken but she was nearing the top. Closer to forgetting Ronald, the dastardly dragon killer. *Speaking of Ronald...*

On cue, a jagged male voice screeched from

below her. Xandie paused for a quick look below. The ocean had swept in, and there was no sign of the demented dragon. "Hope the damn water swallowed you up, Ronald Penne."

"Here's hoping. Otherwise, he'll be on the run from an angry dragon wife for as long as he breathes." A calloused hand attached to a hairy arm dropped into Xandie's vision.

EIGHTEEN

"Come on, Meyers. You need to do more cardio. That cliff climb was pitiful." Chief Zachary Braun grabbed one of Xandie's trembling hands and hauled her to the top of the cliff.

She lay flat on the ground, hugging it and panting. Maybe cranky pants Braun was right. Time to quit hot chocolates and butter puffs. Xandie stared at her nemesis. "How did you know?"

He squinted an electric-blue eye at her. "Let's see, phone call from my mom, text from Melody, frantic call from Es Penne, and a personal visit from an annoyed dragon kidnap victim. Plus, a heads-up from Elspeth." Zack nodded over his shoulder.

Xandie rolled over and scrambled up. Elspeth, in

an emerald green bedazzled jogging suit, sat on top of a crying, skinny bald man.

Her grandmother gave a wave. "Impressive climb, Xandie sweetie. I had feelers out in the underground. A contact gave me a heads-up on this lowlife forget-me-witch who had signed a contract with a dragon by the name of Penne. I tracked him to the clifftop and sat on him until Zachy arrived."

"She flashed me and then immobilized me with a hex. I can't move except to talk and breathe. Do you have any idea how heavy she is?" The bald man shuddered. "I need to forget myself and the last fifteen minutes, including that horrible sight of her flashing me her private areas. No one should remember that." The witch gagged.

"Oh, shush. You should be so lucky." Elspeth grinned and gave Xandie the thumbs-up.

Xandie shook her head at her grandmother's antics. But her thoughts focused on her friend.

"Priss is still down there. We couldn't untie her in time. The tide came in." Xandie fought the sobs crowding her throat. She'd only known the dragon slayer for a short time, but Priss had become a friend. No one, not even Ronald, deserved to drown in a watery grave.

"I wouldn't bet on it." Elspeth cackled. "She still holding her mother's scale?"

"She had it when she visited Marjorie at the police station, why?"

Elspeth pointed.

A whoosh of wind burst past Xandie. Ronald flew screaming into the air before he landed with a meaty splat. Elspeth burst a water balloon over him. He stiffened and went statue still.

She cackled again. "Immobilizing hex bombs. Works on witches and dragons."

Xandie only had eyes for the silvery-pink and sapphire dragon hovering in the air above them. The same dragon that collapsed and shrank to a Priss-sized blonde cheerleader.

Priss bounced up. "Did you see? Can you believe it? Dragon." She punched her arm up. "Hybrids rule."

Running up to Priss, Xandie squeezed her tight in a librarian-dragon-hybrid hug. "How? I...the last thing I saw was the cave filling up."

"I grabbed my mom's scale, and the water swallowed me. There was an electric shock, and I swam out a dragon. I surfaced, and there was old Ronald, clinging to the rock, then whoosh, wings popped out, and here I am."

"Melinda's scales were silvery pink." Marjorie, with the help of Es and Adelind, walked toward them. "You held the scale to your heart. Your mother's last wish would have been to keep you safe. So, the scale did that, and you became a dragon." Marjorie chuckled. "The sapphire color is more water dragons, and that's not a Penne trait, but it saved your life."

Elspeth waved a hand. "But it was a Makepeace trait. I did some research. The Makepeace family have been slayers for decades. But once upon a time, a slayer fell in love with a water dragon. Priss is a combination of both. Wings and fins."

Marjorie stood in front of Priss. "You kept Es and Adelind safe. Most of all, you're my granddaughter, and I can't wait to get to know you." Marjorie folded Priss in a hug both dragons came out of teary eyed.

Zach Braun hauled Ronald and the forget-me-witch upright and snapped cuffs on them. He marched them straight past Xandie but paused to shake his head at her. "Mom filled me in on the last few weeks. You seriously can't keep out of trouble. Are you a body magnet?" He handed his prisoners over to his brothers.

"It's not my fault. Dead bodies just love me," Xandie yelled. As a comeback it sucked, but it was the truth. Priss and her family were safe, the murder solved. The only loose end was her mom's whereabouts. For now, all Xandie could do was hope the troll would turn up some information. And maybe peace and quiet and no bodies for a while.

But this *was* Point Muse. She just hoped the next corpse the town threw at her didn't involve free climbing. Because she really didn't want to give up her hot chocolate...

The End

Book three, The Murderous Monster and the Stony Gaze is available on Amazon now!

NEWSLETTER

Want more?

You can sign up for my mailing list. It's for new releases and no spam. Be the first to grab specials, new releases, and freebies.

Sign up now.
https://www.kellyethan.com/newsletter

ABOUT THE AUTHOR

I want to thank everyone who spent the time to read my novel.

My world is small town magic, mystery and mayhem, with plenty of snarky laughs along the way.

With an overactive imagination and a love of all things that go bump in the night, it was natural to write cozy paranormal mysteries, but I also love paranormal romance. No matter the genre, I love sarcastic heroines who like to save the day and solve the puzzle.

With a busy and chaotic household, writing is my outlet for madness. I live in Australia and when not writing, I can be found plotting my next fictional murder or chasing after the family's ferocious hellhound.

Visit me today at my website or say hello on
Facebook or Twitter.

Website:
https://www.kellyethan.com

Point Muse Cozy Paranormal Mystery Boxed Set: Books 1-3

Point Muse Cozy Paranormal Mystery Boxed Set: Books 4-6

Point Muse Cozy paranormal Mystery Boxed Set: Books 1-8

LILA HARROW: Point Muse Cozy Paranormal Mystery

#1 Cupcakes, Corpses and Chaos

#2 Pies, Potions and Peril

#3 Sin, Sugar and Shadows

Cookies, Curses and Christmas Corpses.

LILA HARROW Point Muse Boxed Set: Books 1-3

HOLLY HARROW: Point Muse Cozy Paranormal Mystery

Banshee, Vikings and Voodoo

#1 Banshee, Death and Disarray

#2 Banshee, Moonshine and Madness

#3 Banshee, Sea Monster and Sabotage

Non Fiction

Heart and Craft.